CANDLELIGHT
Supreme

**"I NEVER DID LIKE TO OBEY THE RULES,"
TY MURMURED AS HE KISSED HER.**

Mary Ellen tried to push Ty away. "Leave me alone!"
she demanded, her face flushed. "You know the rules.
I don't want you to touch me—and I certainly don't
want you to kiss me! Things are over between us,
Ty."

His look was wicked. "What's wrong? Afraid you
won't be able to resist me?"

"That's ridiculous. I'm simply asking you to abide
by the rules. Please don't complicate things."

Running his hands seductively over her back he
smiled. "I'm not trying to complicate things, Mary
Ellen, *you* are. I want to simplify. One bed, instead of
two. And you must know that rules were meant to be
broken. . . ."

CANDLELIGHT SUPREMES

QUANTITY SALES

Most Dell Books are available at special quantity discounts when purchased in bulk by corporations, organizations, and special-interest groups. Custom imprinting or excerpting can also be done to fit special needs. For details write: Dell Publishing Co., Inc., 1 Dag Hammarskjold Plaza, New York, NY 10017, Attn.: Special Sales Dept., or phone: (212) 605-3319.

INDIVIDUAL SALES

Are there any Dell Books you want but cannot find in your local stores? If so, you can order them directly from us. You can get any Dell book in print. Simply include the book's title, author, and ISBN number, if you have it, along with a check or money order (no cash can be accepted) for the full retail price plus 75¢ per copy to cover shipping and handling. Mail to: Dell Readers Service, Dept. FM, P.O. Box 1000, Pine Brook, NJ 07058.

CONTINENTAL LOVER

Cathie Linz

A CANDLELIGHT SUPREME

Published by
Dell Publishing Co., Inc.
1 Dag Hammarskjold Plaza
New York, New York 10017

Copyright © 1986 by Cathie Linz

All rights reserved. No part of this book may be reproduced or transmitted in any form or by any means, electronic or mechanical, including photocopying, recording or by any information storage and retrieval system, without the written permission of the Publisher, except where permitted by law.

Dell ® TM 681510, Dell Publishing Co., Inc.

Candlelight Supreme is a trademark of Dell Publishing Co., Inc.

Candlelight Ecstasy Romance®, 1,203,540, is a registered trademark of Dell Publishing Co., Inc., New York, New York.

ISBN: 0-440-11440-3

Printed in the United States of America

July 1986

10 9 8 7 6 5 4 3 2 1

WFH

Dedicated to those unsung heroines, my editors,
past and present:
Carin Cohen—
For first suggesting I write a Supreme!
Maggie Lichota—
For insisting that I write a Supreme!
Emily Reichert—
For making sure I finished the Supreme!

You've all made writing a pleasure
instead of a job,
so
for all you do, this book's for you!

To Our Readers:

We are pleased and excited by your overwhelmingly positive response to our Candlelight Supremes. Unlike all the other series, the Supremes are filled with more passion, adventure, and intrigue, and are obviously the stories you like best.

In months to come we will continue to publish books by many of your favorite authors as well as the very finest work from new authors of romantic fiction. As always, we are striving to present unique, absorbing love stories —the very best love has to offer.

Breathtaking and unforgettable, Supremes follow in the great romantic tradition you've come to expect *only* from Candlelight Romances.

Your suggestions and comments are always welcome. Please let us hear from you.

Sincerely,

The Editors
Candlelight Romances
1 Dag Hammarskjold Plaza
New York, New York 10017

CONTINENTAL LOVER

CHAPTER ONE

"I need you."

Mary Ellen Campbell stared in disbelief at the only other occupant of the surgical waiting room—the man who had quietly spoken those three words; the man who had been her first lover.

Tyler Stevenson III stood in the shadows, looking very much alone. But then Ty had always been a loner, the rebellious black sheep of the wealthy Stevenson family who had never needed anyone. Surely she couldn't have heard him correctly?

"Marielle, I need you." This time his words were accompanied by an outstretched hand.

Mary Ellen briefly closed her eyes against the deluge of painful memories. She'd been eighteen when a twenty-two-year-old Ty had first called her "Marielle" in that roughly gentle voice of his. At that time she'd been too blindly romantic to believe that Ty had meant it when he'd said he couldn't be tied down.

Mary Ellen hadn't wanted to tie him down; she'd wanted to love him. And she'd wanted him to love her. That summer she'd gotten everything she wanted. But at summer's end Ty had walked away from everything they'd shared.

Now he was back in Chicago again, called home by the news that his father had suffered a heart attack and had to undergo critical heart surgery. Mary Ellen had come to the hospital at the request of Ty's sister, Jennifer. She and Mary Ellen had been good friends since high school and even though Jennifer had married and moved to London last year, the two women kept in close contact.

Mary Ellen thought she'd prepared herself for facing Ty again, but now that she was here she was at a loss. What did one say to the man who had once meant more to her than anyone else in the world? "I'm sorry . . ." she began.

"I don't want your pity," Ty interrupted her, his expression darkening as he dropped his hand back to his side.

"What do you want?"

Mary Ellen half expected him to say, "You." Instead Ty shrugged his shoulders and turned away from her.

She felt his turmoil as if it were her own.

12

Freed from the fear of being caught she allowed herself the luxury of running her eyes over Ty's rangy figure. It had been seven years since she'd last seen him.

Physically the changes weren't many. Ty had always been lean and he still was. But dressed in a dark pullover and jeans he had an intangible aura of strength and authority that had been absent when he was twenty-two. Although styled differently now, Ty's brown hair still had the rebellious tendency to curl slightly; a tendency that had always irritated Ty and delighted Mary Ellen.

Despite the fact that Ty and his father had not been close, or perhaps because of that very fact, the news of Mr. Stevenson's surgery had hit Ty hard. Mary Ellen knew Ty was hurting. She also knew she had to help him. This time she was the one who reached out to him.

"Ty." Her hand was shaking and she could barely speak his name.

Ty slowly turned to face her. He'd always been an expert at masking his expression. But for one brief moment the wall of male invincibility slipped and she viewed the shadow of vulnerability in Ty's dark-brown eyes.

Mary Ellen never knew who took that first step, but seconds later she was in his arms. No longer the footloose playboy; Ty was a man in pain who needed comfort. He cradled her close and she willingly returned the embrace. She was unbearably touched when he accepted her silent offer of support by dropping his head to her shoulder. Biting back the tears Mary Ellen ran soothing fingers through his hair.

There were no sexual overtones in the embrace. This was a time for a more basic human need, the need for understanding and consolation.

But as that need became fulfilled, others began to clamor for attention. Aware of the subtle change, and startled by it, Mary Ellen lifted her face from the inviting softness of Ty's sweater. As she did so, Ty raised his head from her shoulder. Looking up she found herself staring directly at his mouth. Another thing that hadn't changed, she thought to herself with a dazed sense of déjà vu. He still had the most kissable mouth she'd ever seen.

Attempting to remove herself from temptation Mary Ellen slid her hands down to his shoulders and tipped back her head. The movement shifted her line of vision upward to his thickly lashed eyes. Not a very good tactical move on her part, because his eyes were every bit as dangerous as his mouth was.

Ty had sexy eyes. It was as simple as that. Throughout her teenage years she'd spent hours writing flowery passages in her diary trying to describe their exact shade of brown. She'd never even come close. As for describing the very special way he'd looked at her, that, too, had remained elusively out of reach. Even though she hadn't been able to find the words, the feeling itself had never been forgotten, nor repeated. Until now.

Time tumbled backward, erasing the years they'd been apart. Mary Ellen's heart felt as if it had stopped beating. Suddenly she was aware of the warmth of Ty's body beneath his sweater. Her hands had slipped from his shoulders to his chest where her fingers registered the uneven tenor of his breathing.

Slowly, inexorably, the distance between them decreased. She felt the moist warmth of his breath. She saw the flare of passion in his eyes. She heard the huskiness of his voice as he called her "Marielle." Yet still she made no move to evade his hold. Desire held her motionless.

Ty lowered his head and leaned even closer. He was going to kiss her. That realization weakened her knees and sent a rush of excitement chasing through her. There was no mistaking the signals her body was sending to her brain. Ty still had the power to make her want him.

Her common sense struggled to maintain control, but the battle was fierce as his mouth hovered above hers. It took the unexpected arrival of Ty's sister Jennifer to fully bring Mary Ellen to her senses. The interruption broke the spell that had temporarily overwhelmed Mary Ellen, and she hastily stepped away from Ty.

But he had one more thing to say. "Thanks." His voice was a husky caress as he briefly trailed his fingers down her flushed cheek. "I needed that hug." He ran his thumb ever so softly across her lower lip before releasing her.

Mary Ellen turned to face Jennifer, who greeted her with a wan smile. "I'm glad you came. Has there been any word yet?" Jennifer anxiously asked Ty.

Mary Ellen was relieved that Jennifer hadn't noticed the exchange between Ty and herself.

"No word," Ty replied.

"How much longer is it going to be?" Jennifer took an unsteady breath. "Shouldn't we have heard something by now? Do you think something's gone wrong?"

"Take it easy," Mary Ellen said in a soothing voice. "Don't assume the worst."

"I'm just so worried. That's why I called you."

"I know, and I wish there were more that I could do to help."

"Your being here helps," Jennifer told her.

Mary Ellen hugged her good friend and led her over to one of the empty chairs. "Here, sit down before you fall down. How's your mother holding up?"

"We finally convinced her to lie down for a while," Jennifer replied. "She's hardly gotten any sleep since this whole thing started."

The sound of footsteps in the tiled hallway outside the waiting room sent everyone's attention flashing toward the entryway where a man stood, still dressed in his green surgical uniform.

"Dr. Grainger!" The exclamation came from

Jennifer, who jumped to her feet. "How is my father?"

"The surgery went very well. I'd say his chances of recovery are excellent."

"Thank God!" Jennifer began to cry.

Ty awkwardly patted his sister's shoulder. "Have you given my mother the good news?" he asked the doctor.

"Yes, I did. I stopped in to see her before I came here. Your father's in the recovery room now. From there he'll be taken up to the cardiac care unit on the third floor."

"Thank you, Dr. Grainger," Ty said.

The doctor smiled and left the room.

Gratefully accepting the Kleenex Mary Ellen handed her, Jennifer murmured, "I feel so stupid crying now when Dad's going to be fine."

"It's a natural reaction," Mary Ellen reassured her. "Come on, let's go to the ladies' room. A little cold water on your face and you'll be as good as new."

In truth, now that Mary Ellen knew that Mr. Stevenson was going to be all right, she was eager to get away from Ty's unsettling presence. What did he see when he stared at her so intently? Was he remembering her the way she had been at eighteen? Or was he looking at the woman she'd become? Did he notice the changes? Her hair was lighter now than it had been then. She preferred her current look. Did he?

Oh, no, stop right there. Her stern self-directive was accompanied by a negative shake of her head. She wasn't getting involved again. That would be asking for trouble. It would be best to forget that magical moment in his arms. It was only in a moment of weakness that Ty had said he'd needed her. A moment that wouldn't be repeated, she resolutely decided as she ushered Jennifer down the hall to the washroom.

Jennifer took Mary Ellen's advice and rinsed her face with cool water. As she dried her face with a paper towel, Jennifer's eyes met Mary Ellen's in the mirror. "Thanks again for coming to the hospital. I really do appreciate it."

Mary Ellen used a little levity in an attempt to lighten the tension. "Hey, what are friends for? You stayed with me in the emergency room when I broke my wrist."

The ploy worked. Jennifer's smile dispersed the lines of strain around her mouth. "That's because it was my fault you broke your wrist. We were practicing our cheerleading routine, but I was more interested in impressing that quarterback on the football team. What was his name again?"

"Dan Devine."

Jennifer nodded and dug a lipstick out of her purse. "That's right. Dreamy Dan Devine."

"Correction. Make that Dumb Dan Devine. Talking to him was worse than talking to an avocado."

"Who wanted to talk?" Jennifer tossed back with the impish grin she was famous for. Her green eyes flashed with humor as she applied a new coat of lip gloss.

"You're terrible," Mary Ellen reprimanded with the ease of an old friend.

"I know. I felt terrible when I flubbed that tumbling routine and rammed into you. How long did you end up having to wear that cast on your wrist?"

Mary Ellen grimaced as she ran her hairbrush through her wavy, shoulder-length hair. "It seemed like the whole summer."

"I remember Ty made a big production out of writing his life story on your cast."

"He said he wanted to make sure I had some good reading material handy." Mary Ellen's thoughts traveled back to that summer when she'd developed her crush on Ty. At fifteen she'd been thrilled by Ty's dangerous brand of charm. He'd been nineteen and already devilishly experienced in the ways of women. She'd waited three long years for Ty to notice her. And when he finally did, it had taken her seven years to recover from the memories of how good they'd been together.

She didn't want to let herself in for that kind of pain again. Logically she knew as much. But her heart was another matter. Even though she'd tried to prepare herself for meeting Ty again, his actions had caught her completely off guard. Of all the scenarios she'd run through her mind on the way to the hospital, none of them had included his telling her that he needed her.

Jennifer's huge yawn successfully distracted Mary Ellen from her reverie. "You look like you could use some rest," Mary Ellen noted in concern. "Why don't you go on home? You're staying at your parents' house, right?"

Jennifer nodded. "So is Ty. I don't want to leave just yet, though. I want to check in with my mom first. But that doesn't mean you have to stay with me. Go home. I'll be all right now, and I really appreciate your coming." She grimaced ruefully. "I said that already, didn't I?"

"Yes, and you don't want to start repeating yourself," Mary Ellen teased. She waited for Jennifer's answering smile before asking, "Are you sure you don't want me to stay?"

Jennifer nodded. "I'm sure. I'm sorry, though, that you had to come all the way over here just to hold my hand for a while. I hope it wasn't too difficult for you."

"Come on, you make it sound like I trekked in from Outer Mongolia instead of Evanston. I live only twenty minutes from here."

"I know. I wasn't talking about the distance you had to drive, I was talking about you seeing Ty."

"That was over a long time ago." Mary Ellen's strong reassurance was meant as much for herself as for Jennifer. "Don't you worry about me. And you give me a call if you need anything. Someone to talk to, anything."

Jennifer escorted Mary Ellen back to the waiting room to get her coat. Ty was nowhere in sight.

As if reading her mind Jennifer said, "Ty's probably gone to speak to Mom."

"Tell them both good-bye. I'll give you a call tomorrow to see how you're doing, okay?"

"Okay. Drive carefully," Jennifer added as Mary Ellen stepped into the elevator that would take her down to the hospital's main floor. "The roads are slippery."

Mary Ellen told herself that it was foolish to think that Ty might follow her, but she still found herself looking over her shoulder as she made her way to the hospital's main entrance. Once outside, however, the falling snow caused her to focus her attention on reaching the shelter of her car as soon as possible. There was nothing like a Chicago February to put things in their proper prospective!

While the engine warmed up, Mary Ellen got back out of the car and scraped a light coating of snow from the windshield. The snowfall increased as she drove home.

Mary Ellen welcomed the warmth and safety of her apartment as she pulled off her gloves, unwrapped the scarf from around her neck, took off her coat, and tugged off her boots. Padding barefoot into her kitchen, she put the kettle on for a pot of tea.

Twenty minutes later Mary Ellen was sitting on her living-room floor, papers spread out all around her. She'd exchanged the wool paisley skirt and burgundy blouse she'd worn to work and to the hospital for her favorite pair of jeans and a red flannel shirt that was several sizes too large for her. Her feet were still bare, glorying in the freedom of not having to be incarcerated in boots.

The knock on her door startled her, but the identity of her visitor startled her even more.

"Ty!"

"Why did you sneak out on me at the hospital?" he demanded without any preliminaries.

Before Mary Ellen could reply, the telephone rang. She had to abandon her defensive position at the door to go answer it, and Ty followed her into the apartment. He proceeded to make himself at home by removing his snow-speckled coat and carelessly tossing it over a chair. Then he calmly settled down on her couch.

Mary Ellen frowned at Ty as she spoke into the phone. "Hello?"

Apparently some of her disapproval carried over the phone lines, because the caller paused before replying. "Mary Ellen, is that you?" Scott Barnes questioned uncertainly.

"Scott, yes it's me." Mary Ellen made a concerted effort to sound cheerful.

"You sounded so strange when you answered the phone. Is everything all right?"

"Fine."

"Who's Scott?" Ty demanded, making no effort to lower his voice.

"Who was that?" Scott demanded a second later.

"Listen, Scott, let me call you back, okay?" Mary Ellen barely gave Scott time to say okay before hanging up the phone and turning to glare at Ty. He looked entirely too settled in for her peace of mind. He wasn't merely sitting on her couch, he was comfortably sprawled on it as if he belonged there. He was out to make trouble. She knew it as certainly as if he'd written his intentions on a placard. "What do you think you're doing?"

Ty met her anger with provocative calmness. "First things first, Marielle. I'm two questions ahead of you, remember? Why did you sneak out of the hospital, and who is Scott?"

"In the first place I didn't sneak out of the hospital."

"No?" Ty's left eyebrow rose in a mocking gesture of disbelief. "What would you call it?"

"Leaving." She spoke the word succinctly, as if warning Ty that he was in imminent danger of doing the same.

"Without speaking to me first?"

"For your information, Ty, I've been doing a lot of things during the past seven years without speaking to you first." Her voice was saccharine sweet.

"So I hear." He then surprised her by abruptly changing the subject. "I see you still like doing your paperwork on the floor."

"That's right," Mary Ellen acknowledged somewhat defensively before gathering up the reports she'd been working on and carefully placing them on her glass-and-oak coffee table.

"Jen tells me that you've turned into a noble humanitarian."

23

"I seriously doubt that your sister put it quite like that," Mary Ellen retorted.

"But you are involved with some kind of lofty charity work aren't you?"

Mary Ellen shook her head in exasperation. "You make me sound like a cross between Robin Hood and Joan of Arc. I happen to work for a worldwide, nonprofit organization called Hunger Prevention. I'm a project coordinator, which means that I organize the efforts of various groups interested in ending world hunger."

"Is that how you met Scott?" Ty neatly inserted.

"That's really none of your business."

"I'm making it my business."

"Too bad," she shot back with impatient bluntness. "My answer is still the same. You've got no right barging in here and prying into my personal life."

"So Scott's part of your personal life, is he?" Ty's tone sounded ominous. He obviously was not pleased with the news.

Mary Ellen struggled to hang on to her temper. "Look, Ty, I know you've had a rough day. I don't want to get into a fight with you."

"Good, because I don't want to fight with you either," he concurred.

Mary Ellen's relief was short lived: Ty lowered his voice and added a seductive postscript. "I want to make love to you, I want to feel you melting in my arms when I make you mine."

That did it! Mary Ellen's anger exploded. "You've got one hell of a nerve, you know that?"

Ty was unfazed by the obvious light of battle in her eyes. Instead he had the nerve to send her a knowing smile of satisfaction. "I'd forgotten how beautiful you are when you're angry."

"You've forgotten more than that," Mary Ellen said with arctic frigidity. "You've also forgotten that our affair was over a long time ago!"

"Care to test my memory, Marielle?"

Mary Ellen didn't like the sound of his husky challenge at all. Or maybe she liked it too much. She couldn't be sure, but either way her protective instincts raced to the fore and sounded their alarm. "I don't care to test anything you have to offer, thank you." She was rather pleased at how decisive she sounded. That was good—at least her inner ambivalence wasn't outwardly apparent.

Ty, however, looked beyond outward appearances. He took his sweet time studying her, and there was nothing academic about his appraisal. First he focused his attention on her eyes. Not only did she have the bluest eyes he'd ever seen, they were also the most expressive. Beneath the frosty anger was uncertainty, and something else which encouraged him to look further.

His gaze shifted to the layered angle of bangs that her slender fingers were nervously shoving away from her eyes. The light from a chrome lamp illuminated streaks of pure gold in her light-brown hair. Then his eyes lowered past her curvy mouth and stubborn chin to the rapid rise and fall of her breasts evident beneath her red flannel shirt.

"I still get to you, don't I." It wasn't a question, it was a statement of fact.

"I think you'd better leave," Mary Ellen announced.

Ty obligingly got to his feet. But he had no intention of leaving.

"Forget it," she warned him, having read his intentions in the expectant gleam in his eyes. "I'm not going to allow you to waltz back into my life again. No way!" She took two steps backward for each of his steps forward. "Are you listening to me?" she shouted as he continued to stalk her. "This isn't some kind of game. You dropped out of my life seven years ago and you can stay out of it. It's over!"

"Over, Marielle?" He caught her in his arms and lowered his mouth to hers. "It's just beginning." The words were spoken against her lips seconds before he kissed her.

CHAPTER TWO

Mary Ellen knew she was in trouble the moment his lips touched hers. For once her memory had actually served her incorrectly. His kiss was even *more* tantalizing than she'd remembered!

She struggled against the whirlpool of pleasure that threatened to tow her under, but the pressure of his mouth on hers continued to be frankly possessive and fiercely consuming. His hunger succeeded in stealing the last remnants of her anger and replacing it with a need as intense as his own.

Her hands, which had been raised to ward him off, now slid around his waist. The stiffness that had held her immobile gave way to a melting warmth. And her mouth, which had been tight with anger, softened.

Ty quickly changed his own approach. No longer was his kiss overwhelmingly possessive. He now displayed wooing tenderness and teasing charm. Her lips parted beneath his and greeted the thrust of his tongue with fervent abandon.

Tasting her response Ty pulled her even closer. His hands explored her body as thoroughly as his tongue was exploring her mouth. He soon deserted the flannel material of her shirt in favor of the infinitely softer skin beneath it. The feel of his fingers caressing her bare skin made Mary Ellen dizzy. *Or perhaps it was lack of oxygen that was causing that,* she thought to herself with hazy wonder.

Ty's next move challenged that theory. His lips reluctantly parted from hers, but the dizziness she was experiencing wasn't diminished any by the deep breaths of air she drew in. Heady excitement continued to course through her as his fingers performed a slow ascent of her spine. He dropped a matching kiss to the outline of her mouth for every millimeter he moved his hands.

His kisses soon wandered across her face to launch a seductive attack on the sensitive skin of her earlobe, an erogenous zone that Ty had been the first to discover. Now he returned to take advantage of that knowledge. Between tiny love-bites his tongue traced erotic circles along the shell-like curve of her ear.

Mary Ellen was so steeped in delectable sensations that it took her a moment to realize that the back fastening of her bra was insidiously being undone by skillful fingers. The release of the restraining garment brought with it a return to the reality of her situation. Despite her heated response Mary Ellen wasn't prepared for things to proceed any farther. She'd never intended for them to come this far!

She opened eyes clouded with passion and forced the word *"No"* past her well-kissed lips. Her second denial was much more forceful and succeeded in gaining Ty's attention.

"What's wrong?"

"Let me go." She struggled against his hold.

Seeing the determination on her face Ty reluctantly released her.

Mary Ellen put as much distance between them as possible before answering. "You've proved your point—the physical attraction between us isn't dead. But that doesn't mean anything. There are more important things at issue here."

"Name one," he challenged her.

"I need to know why. Why now? Why disappear from my life for seven years without ever bothering to get in touch with me? Why try to rekindle things between us again? Because you're in Chicago and I'm handy?"

"No."

"Then why?"

"Keeping in touch would only have made things harder."

"For you, or for me?"

"For both of us." He closed the distance between them. "I was always up front with you, Marielle. I warned you I'd be leaving at the end of that summer."

"And now?"

"Now you fill an emptiness inside me that I wasn't even aware existed. When I saw you for the first time at the hospital, I knew that what was missing in my life was you. You're more beautiful now than you were at eighteen, you know that?" He traced his fingers across her face.

Mary Ellen had no illusions about her looks. Her nose was too upturned and her chin too stubborn to qualify for classic beauty. When put all together the sum of the parts created a face that was alive and vibrant, but it wasn't a face that would launch any ships.

"Stop looking so disbelieving," he softly reprimanded her. "I may not have contacted you since that summer we were together, but that doesn't mean I ever forgot about you. You're not the kind of woman a man can forget, Marielle."

"Apparently I'm not the kind he remembers, either." Her observation was bittersweet.

"That's not true. Shall I tell you what I remember, Marielle? I remember your soap, your favorite color, your lucky number, exactly how long you like to soak in a hot tub. I remember how you loved me. I also remember that you'd only just turned eighteen and were barely out of high school."

"I'm not eighteen anymore," she pointed out in a husky voice. "So where do we go from here?"

"Out to dinner."

Mary Ellen shook her head. Uncertainty was evident in her blue eyes. "I don't know. . . ."

"I do. Say yes."

"Ty, I don't want to get in over my head again. I don't even know how long you'll be staying in Chicago."

"I'll stay as long as it takes for my father to recover and for you to go out with me."

"And once I agree to go out with you? What then?"

"So many questions, Marielle." He delivered a teasing tap to the tip of her upturned nose. "We have a much better chance of answering them together than we do apart." His touch turned into a caress. "What do you say?"

Tempted though she was, Mary Ellen resolutely maintained her hold on reality. Once again she stepped away from Ty and the spell he was casting on her senses. "I say let's wait until tomorrow and see how things look in the cold light of day. This has been an emotional day for both of us."

Surprisingly Ty agreed to her decision. "Okay. But I can tell you one thing. Matters will look the same tomorrow as they do tonight."

He stole another kiss before he gathered his

coat and said good-night. After he'd gone, Mary Ellen lifted trembling fingers to her mouth. She could still taste him on her lips.

Now she knew why she'd been unable to make a commitment to Scott Barnes, the man she'd been dating for the past few months. Scott was a good man; stable, hardworking, reliable. But he'd never made her feel the way Ty had, and Mary Ellen knew it wasn't fair to either herself or Scott to accept anything less. Breaking the news to Scott was not an easy task, as she discovered when she returned his call a few minutes later.

"I'm sorry I was so abrupt earlier," Mary Ellen apologized, "but I had company."

Scott got right to the point. "Was it that guy you used to go with, the one who's back in town to see his sick father?"

Mary Ellen had been honest about her past. She'd never lied to Scott and she wasn't about to begin now. "Yes."

"I see."

"Scott, I—"

"You don't have to say it, Mary Ellen. I knew you were carrying a torch for the guy, but I'd hoped you'd get over it. From what you've told me about him, it doesn't sound like he can offer you anything, Mary Ellen. What is he, some kind of race-car driver? Hardly a stable profession. In fact, it's downright dangerous."

Strangely enough Mary Ellen wasn't worried about Ty's racing. Reckless though he might be in all other aspects of his life, he'd always been an excellent driver. "Ty is very good at what he does."

"Including making love?"

"Scott!"

"That's what you were thinking, isn't it?"

Mary Ellen stubbornly refused to answer that question.

Scott swore softly before relenting. "I just don't want to see you hurt, honey."

"I know that, Scott. And I don't want you to be hurt either. But I'm just not ready to settle down yet. Don't you see, I'm thinking about your best interests too. You deserve someone who can love you without any reservations. Unfortunately I'm not that someone. I'm sorry."

"Me too. I hope you know what you're doing, Mary Ellen. You've been burned once by this guy. Be careful."

Mary Ellen mulled over Scott's advice as she prepared for bed. Being careful was difficult where Ty was concerned. She had a weakness for him that seemed to be unaffected by the passage of time.

When she finally fell asleep her dreams picked up where reality had left off, continuing the sensual fantasy of Ty's lovemaking. Just when things were reaching their ultimate conclusion, the sound of the ringing telephone abruptly shattered her imminent fulfillment and brought her out of her deep sleep.

Mary Ellen glared at the telephone sitting on her bedside table. The instrument showed no sign of remorse at its inopportune interruption.

"Hello?"

"My, we're crabby this morning," Ty commented, his voice carrying clearly through the phone's receiver.

"Ty! Is something wrong? Your father—?"

"Is doing well. Nothing is wrong."

"Then why are you calling me at"—Mary Ellen squinted at her digital clock—"five fifty-nine in the morning?"

"I'm following instructions. Last night you said to 'wait until tomorrow and see how things look in the cold light of day.' Well, it may not be light yet, but it is cold and it is tomorrow. Visiting hours at the hospital are over at seven-thirty tonight, so I'll pick you up at eight. Just say yes."

Mary Ellen shoved her hair out of her eyes. Not yet fully awake she gave in and mumbled, "Yes."

"You won't regret it, Marielle," Ty promised softly.

Mary Ellen regretted it the moment she hung up the phone. She continued to regret it at odd moments throughout her day at work. A phone call to Jennifer helped take her mind off her predicament.

"I got to see Dad this morning," Jennifer told Mary Ellen. "It was pretty frightening to see all those tubes connected to him, but he seems in good spirits and the doctors are very pleased with his recovery."

34

"I'm glad," Mary Ellen replied. "Is there anything I can do?"

"You're doing plenty already. The flowers you sent Dad are lovely. And Ty mentioned that you'd taken pity on him and were going out to dinner with him tonight. I'm glad he's taking a little time off to unwind. Dad's attack and the surgery hit Ty pretty hard."

"I know." What Mary Ellen didn't know was how large a factor nostalgia played in Ty's interest in her now. During an emotional crisis it was natural to turn to someone who'd once been close to you, but it was only a temporary condition.

Wondering what she was letting herself in for Mary Ellen prepared for her date that evening with a sense of wary trepidation. She was ready and waiting when Ty rang her doorbell at five to eight.

He held a single red carnation in his hand. "For you."

"Thank you and come in," she nervously invited him. "I'll just go put this in a vase."

By the time Mary Ellen had returned to the living room with a vase from the kitchen, she'd recovered some measure of her composure. So Ty had remembered her weakness for carnations—that was no reason to go off the deep end. Too bad she couldn't completely convince herself of that.

Of course the way he looked at her didn't help any. He was practically devouring her with his eyes. Mary Ellen self-consciously smoothed her wool skirt and raised a hand to straighten the already-straight rolled collar of her angora sweater. Unable to stand the suspense any longer she finally said, "Is something wrong?"

"Nothing. I was just looking at you."

She corrected him on his choice of words. "Staring. You were staring at me."

To which he simply replied, "You're worth staring at."

"So are you."

Ty had the type of physique that was made for the elegance of a suit. Actually he was dangerously attractive whatever he wore. Everything looked good on him. Then Mary Ellen recalled that he looked even better wearing nothing at all!

"I hate to break up this mutual admiration society," Ty murmured, wondering at the flush coloring Mary Ellen's face. "But we'd better get on our way or we'll be late for our reservations." He picked up her coat and held it open invitingly.

"Where are we going this evening?" she asked as she slid her arms into it. At least her voice still worked, even if it did sound somewhat shaky.

Ty gently freed her hair from beneath the coat collar. "You'll see."

He took her to a North Side restaurant that had recently opened and gotten great reviews from the food editors of *Chicago* magazine.

"Confess," he insisted over their appetizer of

artichoke fritters. "You thought I was going to take you to one of our former haunts, didn't you?"

"That thought did cross my mind."

"Mine too. But looking back I realized that we actually frequented the clubs around here more than we did the classy restaurants."

"I guess that's true. Are you still a devoted fan of bluegrass music?"

"Of course. Some things never change." The deep softness of his voice wrapped her in its warmth. An echoing heat was being generated by his sensual contemplation of her mouth.

"It's Friday night, and I happen to know that several good bands are performing tonight. Are you interested?"

Mary Ellen nodded. She'd gone past being interested a few seconds ago and had advanced to being dangerously close to fascinated!

After dinner they made the rounds of the bluegrass hot spots. It was nearing two-thirty in the morning when Ty gallantly took the key from Mary Ellen's fingers and opened her apartment door for her.

"How about a hot cup of coffee?" she asked as she removed her coat.

"Sounds good."

It didn't take Mary Ellen long to prepare two mugs full of steaming Irish Mint-flavored coffee. At the last minute she decided to add a dollop of whipped cream for good measure.

That proved to be her downfall, because Ty teasingly insisted on licking the whipped-cream mustache from her lips each time she took a sip of coffee. Soon the coffee and the whipped cream were both forgotten as Ty concentrated on the more rewarding taste of her mouth.

His kisses ranged from soft tenderness to hungry passion and encompassed all the countless nuances in between. He kissed her lips . . . her cheeks . . . her eyes.

Moving with unhurried skill Ty slid his hand down her back. He stroked her in a petting motion that was both soothing and exciting. Mary Ellen looped her arms around his neck and leaned closer, unintentionally intensifying the intimacy of their embrace. As she became aware of his increasing arousal, her body yielded to accommodate his.

"Marielle, feel what you do to me. It was always like this between us, remember?" His voice was raspy as he spoke.

She nodded.

The movement drew his attention to the curve of her throat. When the collar of her sweater obstructed his caresses, he nudged it aside and continued nibbling his way down to her collarbone. There he teased her with the tip of his tongue. Easing her away from him Ty stared down at her bemused face. "Tell me you want me the way I want you."

His demand brought her to her senses. "It's too soon," Mary Ellen whispered, frightened by how completely she'd gone under his spell. "This is happening too fast for me! Yesterday

38

morning I didn't even know you were back in this country. We've been apart a long time. You don't even know me anymore."

"What I don't know, I'm willing to learn. Are you willing to try?" He took her hand and raised it to his lips. "Give it a chance, Marielle."

She did give it a chance by agreeing to see Ty frequently throughout the next two weeks. At first she was hesitant, leery of getting hurt again. But her caution was soon diminished by her happiness at being with Ty again. He was courting her as he'd never done before, taking her out for romantic dinners, escorting her to a play she'd mentioned wanting to see, whisking her off to the newest nightspots. And at the end of each evening their kisses became more passionate, their embraces more intimate.

Inevitably Mary Ellen began to hope that this renewed relationship might have a chance after all. She said as much to Jennifer when the two women met for lunch one Saturday afternoon.

"Ty has opened up to me in a way he never did when we were younger."

"That's encouraging. I have to say that you look radiant." Jennifer's smile held a gleam of satisfaction as she added, "Ty's been looking pretty pleased with himself too."

"Really?" Mary Ellen was glad to hear that. "Of course Ty often looks pleased with himself, it doesn't necessarily have anything to do with me."

"I think it has everything to do with you,"

Jennifer stated, just as Mary Ellen had hoped she would. "Like I said, Dad's surgery really hit Ty hard. I wasn't expecting Ty to just put everything on hold and fly home like this. The fact that he did shows how much he really does care. Ty's like that, you know, always has been. He rarely says what he's really feeling. But you can tell by his actions, and by his behavior. And let me tell you, his behavior lately points to his being hung up on you." Jennifer paused and sighed dramatically. "Having so much romance brewing around me makes me miss my husband."

"Here you go, ladies." The waitress interrupted them to deposit a three-inch-high pizza on the table and efficiently slice it for them. "Enjoy."

"Thanks," Mary Ellen replied.

After she and Jennifer had served themselves, Jennifer spoke again. "Now, where was I?"

"You were telling me how much you miss your husband and I was going to tell you about a surprise I've got planned."

"You were? What kind of surprise? Come on, come on, tell me," Jennifer demanded. "You know I hate surprises. Well, actually I love them, but I hate waiting to find out what they are. Tell me!"

"I will if you'll give me half a chance," Mary Ellen retorted with a grin. "I would have told you earlier, but you've been so worried about your father's health that the opportunity didn't arise." Seeing Jennifer's impatient expression and rolling eyes, Mary Ellen laughed and got right to the point. "I'm finally going to take you up on the invitation to the Ritz you've been handing me ever since you moved to London. I'm coming to England!"

Jennifer looked delighted. "Are you kidding?"

"No. Remember that bus tour I told you about in my last letter?"

"The one that goes all over Europe?"

"That's the one. I've signed up for it. The tour leaves in mid-April and our first stop is London."

"That's great! How long will you be staying?"

"We only have a day or so in London and then we move on to Copenhagen."

"We'll have to celebrate your first trip to London with tea at the Ritz, just like I promised," Jennifer declared. "I'll make reservations as soon as I get back."

"Are you leaving soon?"

Jennifer nodded. "Dad's doing so much better now that I decided to book my return flight for Wednesday evening. I phoned Ian last night with the flight number. We talked for over an hour. He misses me as much as I miss him."

"Sounds like Ian's turned out to be a devoted husband."

"He's the best." Jennifer finished her last slice of pizza. "Now, tell me, where else is this bus tour of yours going?"

"From London we fly to Copenhagen and

then take the bus south across Germany and Austria. I can't remember all the places where we stop. Then we head over to Paris and Brussels before returning to London to fly home."

"How long is this marathon?"

"Two weeks."

"Wear comfortable shoes," Jennifer advised. "And bring a pillow to sit on in the bus."

"Any other words of wisdom for my first trip to Europe?" Mary Ellen inquired.

"Just to enjoy yourself. You deserve it."

As Mary Ellen waited for Ty to pick her up that evening, she studied the tour itinerary and brochures she'd received from her travel agent in the afternoon mail. Ty was running a bit late and she was beginning to get worried when her doorbell finally rang.

Ty had told her to wear something special. She hoped the royal-blue silk brocade dress qualified. She wore her hair up, held there by a pair of matching cloisonné combs.

Upon opening her door she discovered that Ty was not alone.

"Surprise!" Ty announced before briskly whisking her aside so that the waiters standing beside him could bring in the boxes they were holding.

"What's going on?" Mary Ellen demanded in confusion.

Ty pointed at Mary Ellen's dining-room table and began giving instructions to the two men. "Just set things up over there. The kitchen's through here. You can go ahead and get started."

"Wait a second! Who are these guys?" Mary Ellen was so stunned that she hadn't even closed her apartment door yet.

Ty released the doorknob from her fingers and shut the door for her. "You have been chosen as the lucky recipient of a personally catered, post-Valentine dinner for two. Congratulations, Marielle."

"Post-Valentine's Day?"

"Regretfully I wasn't here for that romantic day, so I thought we'd celebrate it tonight. Wait till you see what's on the menu. Hearts of palm salad, goose with passion-fruit sauce, and for dessert—chocolate meringue kisses. But first, a cocktail." Ty led Mary Ellen over to the dining-room table, which had been miraculously transformed in the space of a few minutes. A pink damask tablecloth now covered its surface while bone china, silver flatware, and crystal stemware created a setting for two. Pink candles, already lit, stood in elegant silver candle holders. The pièce de résistance was the centerpiece, a sterling silver bowl holding a fresh bouquet of pink carnations, fern, and baby's breath.

Mary Ellen was overwhelmed. "Ty, it's lovely!"

"I'm glad you like it. It's got to be back by midnight," he informed her with a grin, "but till then it's all ours. Ah, here's our cocktail."

One of the waiters came out of the kitchen

43

carrying a silver tray with two delicate champagne glasses upon it.

"Thanks," Mary Ellen murmured as the white-gloved waiter handed her a drink. "Mmmm, this is delicious. What is it?"

"Champagne and raspberry liqueur," Ty answered, his voice softly seductive. "It's called the First Kiss."

The cocktail set the mood for the ensuing feast. The waiters served them with discreet efficiency. When Mary Ellen and Ty were finished eating, they retired to the living room for coffee while the waiters packed everything back up and departed.

"They left the centerpiece," Mary Ellen noted as she set her coffee cup on the end table.

"It's yours," Ty replied, setting his cup beside hers. "And so am I."

Ty's kisses were seductive. He wooed her with gentle nibbles that tempted her to return his evocative play. She did. Her lips skimmed over his, sweeping back and forth, always touching but never settling.

However, when her teeth boldly toyed with his lower lip, Ty moaned—and the mood shifted from playful to passionate. His mouth captured hers for a kiss that was fiercely consuming, his tongue seeking and easily gaining admission to the inner softness of her mouth. Mary Ellen shivered and drew him closer. Her fingers dug into his shoulders and wrinkled the fine material of his suit jacket.

44

Without lifting his lips from hers Ty eased Mary Ellen down onto the couch. From this recumbent position a new host of temptations became evident. Mary Ellen felt the heat of his body from her shoulders to her thighs. As one kiss blended into the next, Ty shifted so that she was sensuously molded against him.

Impatient of the barriers still between them Mary Ellen peeled his jacket away from his shoulders. The buttons of his shirt were her next target. As soon as each one was parted from its buttonhole, she greeted his bared skin with the tip of her fingernail. Soon the powerful expanse of Ty's entire chest was available to her caressing hands.

By this time Ty's kisses had wandered from her mouth down to the base of her throat. As Mary Ellen's hands were exploring him, so, too, were his exploring her. They slid inside the collar of her dress to caress the nape of her neck, the curve of her shoulder. Moments later he'd skillfully undone the front fastening of her dress. The material easily succumbed to his bidding, revealing the lavender lace of her bra.

Ty looked down at her with eyes that spoke of his needs and desires. "You're so beautiful," he whispered.

He reached out to touch her gently with his fingertip, evocatively tracing the lacy demicups of her lingerie. The firm slopes of her breasts swelled with pleasure as he nibbled at her flesh through the sheer fabric, tantalizing her, exciting her, until her sighs became sultry moans. Only then did Ty finally undo the front fastening of her bra, revealing her beautiful naked breasts.

He caressed her as if she were a priceless work of art and he an awed artist. He seduced her with words and with actions. Whispering his erotic intentions Ty lowered his head and drew the tip of her breast into his mouth. He exulted in the creamy taste of her skin.

The tugging motion of his mouth and the velvety caress of his tongue sent a molten flow of ecstasy rippling through her. Adrift in a sea of pleasure Mary Ellen anchored her fingers in the vibrant thickness of his hair and held him closer.

Wanting to return some of the intense pleasure he was giving her, Mary Ellen slid one hand beneath his loose shirt. She remembered where he liked to be touched, and she visited those places now—the curve of his waist, the small of his back. She touched her lips to the top of his head and smiled as the raking motion of her fingernails across his bare flesh caused him to shudder with desire.

Releasing her from his enticing hold Ty spoke in a raspy undertone. "Put your arms around my neck."

She obeyed but asked, "Why?"

He kissed her lips before answering. "Because I'm going to carry you to bed."

Before Mary Ellen had time to comprehend fully what he'd told her, Ty was once again spreading kisses across her face as he pulled himself up into a sitting position and brought her with him. Thanks to his maneuvering she ended up draped across his lap. Ty had planned it that way so that he could carry her easier, but he found that once she was actually perched so close he couldn't resist pausing to enjoy the lips she so readily offered him.

Ty's arousal was obvious. Mary Ellen's heated response only served to further inflame his already sorely tried self-control. Scooping her in his arms Ty fairly launched himself off the couch. By the time she opened her passion-dazed eyes, Ty had already carried her down the hallway to her bedroom. As he dropped her to the bed and began stripping off his shirt, Mary Ellen came to her senses with unwelcome speed.

"Ty, wait." She sat up and held out a trembling hand. "We need to talk."

"We'll talk afterward." He tossed his shirt aside and started unfastening his slacks.

"No!" In an effort to gain his attention Mary Ellen had spoken more forcefully than she'd intended.

"No?" Ty repeated in disbelief. "What do you mean no?"

"Ty . . . we have to talk."

His expression was dark with impatience and masculine frustration. "Marielle, I didn't bring you into the bedroom to talk! Up until a minute ago you were with me all the way. Now you've suddenly turned the passion off. What is this, some kind of game with you?"

"I'm not playing games," she denied angrily. "I just think we need to talk."

But Ty had already gathered his shirt and was in the process of leaving. "Not now. You may be able to turn on and off at will, but I can't. If I stay here I'm going to finish what we started."

"Ty . . ."

"I'm only human, Marielle." He spoke in a harsh tone. "We'll talk later."

He walked out, and a moment later Mary Ellen heard the door to her apartment slam shut. He'd gone.

Damn! Of all the rotten times for her to get cold feet. Mary Ellen shoved her hair out of her eyes. The cloisonné haircombs had long since fallen out, unable to withstand the force of Ty's caressing fingers. Just as she had been unable to resist the passionate power of Ty's lovemaking. But while he may have overcome her physical reservations, her mental reservations had needed something more. She'd needed to hear some kind of verbal reassurance that this would be more than a one-night stand for him. She needed to know that they'd be sharing something important, and not casually having sex for "old times' sake."

Mary Ellen knew she hadn't expressed herself well or handled the situation very adeptly, but then Ty hadn't reacted well either. He hadn't given her time to recover her wits long enough to make a rational explanation, but she intended to rectify that first thing in the morning. She'd call Ty and tell him exactly why she'd reacted the way she had. She'd be honest and candid about her needs. Then it would be up to Ty.

Unfortunately the Stevensons' phone line was busy when Mary Ellen dialed it first thing the next morning. She kept trying for an hour. Frustrated, she decided to run some quick errands and then try to reach Ty again when she came back to her apartment.

As is usually the case with errands, they took longer than Mary Ellen had anticipated. When she returned home she found an envelope stuck halfway under the welcome mat that sat in the hallway in front of her apartment door.

"What's this?" She leaned down and scooped up the unexpected missive. It was a brief note from Ty. *I'll be in touch,* he'd written. But when?

She called the Stevensons' home to find out.

"Jennifer? It's Mary Ellen. Is Ty there?"

"No, he's not."

"When do you expect him back?"

"I'm not sure." Jennifer sounded upset. "Ty went back to Europe."

"Europe!" Mary Ellen could actually feel the blood drain from her face.

"That's right. He said something important had come up. He left this morning; took a flight to New York and is getting a connection from there. He told me he tried to call you, but that no one was home. He said he'd drop by your place on his way to the airport, and that if you

49

still weren't home he'd leave a note. Didn't you find it?"

"I found it." Mary Ellen looked down at the brief note she still held in her hand. "I just didn't understand it at first," she whispered in a choked voice. "I do now."

"Maybe it's not as bad as it seems," Jennifer tried to reassure her.

"It's not bad at all, it's for the best."

"Are you all right?" Jennifer asked, concerned by Mary Ellen's hardened determination.

"I will be. Thanks, Jennifer. Bye."

I'll be in touch, Ty had casually written. Mary Ellen crumpled the note and threw it away, passionately vowing that Tyler Stevenson III would never touch her again!

CHAPTER THREE

"What happens if I cancel my trip to Europe?" Mary Ellen asked her travel agent over the phone first thing Monday morning.

"There is a cancellation fee, the amount varies depending on when you cancel. Why? Is something wrong? You're not getting cold feet, are you?"

Pam Warner had become Mary Ellen's friend as well as her travel agent, so Mary Ellen felt compelled to make some kind of explanation. "I'm just not sure I want to go to Europe."

"Why not?" Pam asked her. "You've been looking forward to this trip for ages."

"I was looking forward to it, yes, but I'm not anymore." Mary Ellen's voice was low as she confessed, "I really don't feel like taking a trip and living it up right now. I'm not in the mood to enjoy it."

"That doesn't sound like you. Come on, Mary Ellen, what gives?" Pam was concerned. "There must be more to this than just a case of the blues."

"You're right, this is more than just a case of the blues," Mary Ellen replied. "This is full-fledged depression." She sighed and twisted the phone cord around her fingers. "Part of the problem is that Europe just doesn't hold very good connotations for me at the moment. Someone I know, and would rather not meet again, has gone back there and I don't want to run into him."

"Don't worry about it," Pam advised her in a soothing voice. "The chances of you running into anyone you know are one in million. There's a much better chance that you'll meet someone new and exciting who'll make you forget this jerk you're trying to avoid."

The idea of being able to forget Ty was very appealing to Mary Ellen, especially after two nights of being haunted by his image. The tantalizing sampling she'd had of his lovemaking had only evoked a terrible craving for more. But Mary Ellen was determined not to give in to her addiction for Ty. She *would* get over him and forget him.

"Mary Ellen?" Pam prompted. "What's it going to be? Are you going to let this guy ruin your vacation for you?"

"Absolutely not. You're right, Pam. He's

ruined enough, I won't allow him to ruin this too!"

"That's the spirit," Pam applauded. "Now, give me a call again if you start having any more doubts."

"I will," Mary Ellen promised.

Mary Ellen had barely hung up the phone when it began to ring. "Hello?"

"Oh, good!" Jennifer exclaimed. "I'm glad I caught you before you left for work."

"Something wrong?" Mary Ellen asked.

"No, I just wanted to say that I hope you won't let whatever happened between you and Ty affect our friendship."

Mary Ellen fought the sudden urge to cry. "Hey, we've been friends too long for *anything* to ruin our friendship."

"I'm glad to hear that. I didn't want to be guilty by association, or in this case, guilty by relation," Jennifer murmured wryly.

"You can't help the fact that Ty is your brother, and you can't control his actions. No one can," Mary Ellen added bitterly. "I should have known better. I'm angry at myself and at Ty, but not at you."

"So we're still on for tea at the Ritz?" Jennifer asked, hoping to divert Mary Ellen's attention to a more pleasant topic.

"Sure thing." Mary Ellen was just as eager to avoid further mention of Ty. "And my offer to take you to the airport still stands."

"In that case I'll accept, thanks."

"Fine. Tell me when I should pick you up."

Mary Ellen hurriedly scribbled down Jennifer's reply and the particulars of her flight. "I'll be there." Catching a glimpse of the time displayed on her watch, Mary Ellen groaned. "Uh-oh. I'd better get moving here, or I'm going to be late for work."

Throughout that day and the next Mary Ellen successfully banished Ty from her mind by inundating herself with work. She was coordinating a matching-grant program from a multinational corporation based in Chicago. She was also organizing efforts by several community groups that were engaging in various activities: benefit concerts, craft sales, fashion shows engineered to raise money. She went home so tired at night that it took all of her remaining energy to stick a frozen dinner in the oven and eat it while reviewing the progress reports of Hunger Prevention's various fund-raising activities before falling into bed.

On Wednesday, Mary Ellen went from work directly to Jennifer's parents' home in the exclusive Chicago suburb of Lake Forest. She arrived a few minutes early. Looking at the stately three-story Georgian brick house, Mary Ellen was visibly reminded of the difference between her own middle-class upbringing and Jennifer's very upper-class background. Had the two girls not attended the same parochial high school, their paths would never have crossed and Mary Ellen would never have been introduced to Jennifer's reckless older brother. Such was fate.

Mary Ellen had known many moments both of happiness and sadness at this house. She and Jennifer had practiced their high-school cheerleading routines on the spacious front lawn. They'd spent their summers tanning themselves beside the swimming pool in the back. And they'd once had to clean all the windows on the main floor of the house as punishment for releasing a dozen goldfish into that same swimming pool!

Mary Ellen hadn't visited the house since Jennifer's wedding last year. She'd been afraid she'd run into Ty then, but he'd sent his regrets; something to do with a conflict with his racing schedule. Jennifer had teasingly said that Ty's real reason for avoiding the celebration was his aversion to matrimony.

Everyone had laughed, except for Mary Ellen, who knew that Ty's aversion wasn't merely to matrimony, it was to commitment of any kind—which was why his reckless, fast-paced life-style suited him so perfectly. He never stayed in one place for long. She should have learned her lesson at eighteen.

"Those who forget their mistakes are doomed to repeat them," Mary Ellen muttered to herself as she got out of her car. "And I don't aim to make any more mistakes."

Determined to make Jennifer's departure a pleasant one, Mary Ellen was deliberately cheerful, but the act didn't fool her old friend one bit. Even now, as Mary Ellen stood in line beside Jennifer at the British Airways ticket desk at the airport, she was making every effort to hide her melancholy behind a teasing patter of conversation.

A concerned Jennifer saw through the act and noted the lack of laughter in Mary Ellen's eyes, the dark shadows beneath those eyes.

"We've got some time before my flight leaves," Jennifer said after she'd checked her luggage. "How about a drink?"

"Sure."

The stand-up bar in the international terminal was crowded, so Mary Ellen and Jennifer took their wine spritzers and moved out into the general waiting area.

"Before you know it, you'll be standing here waiting for your flight to be called," Jennifer noted. "Are you getting excited about your trip?"

Mary Ellen nodded and took another sip of her drink.

"Remember that it can be cold in London in April, so be sure to bring enough warm clothing."

Mary Ellen smiled. "You're speaking to someone who's lived in Chicago all their life, remember? Chicago, the city with the old adage—If you don't like our weather, stick around for a minute, it's bound to change. I've learned to cope with changeable weather."

"I think you've also learned to cope with changeable people, like my brother. I really thought that this time you two would get together and stay that way. I'm sorry things

56

worked out the way they have," Jennifer murmured.

Mary Ellen's smile slipped. She didn't want to talk about Ty, she couldn't. It was still much too painful. Determined not to lose control she quickly changed the subject. "At least your father is well on the road to recovery. That's good news."

Jennifer nodded in agreement. She wanted to say more about Ty, but the desperation in Mary Ellen's eyes made her hesitate. A moment later the sound of Jennifer's flight being called took the matter out of her hands and prevented them from discussing things further.

"Here, don't forget your tote bag." Mary Ellen handed Jennifer the piece of designer luggage. "Have you got your boarding pass?"

"Right here." Jennifer gave Mary Ellen a farewell hug. "Take care of yourself and write."

"You too." Mary Ellen blinked away her tears. "I'll see you in London."

Exactly one month later Mary Ellen returned to the international terminal of Chicago's O'Hare Airport and stood waiting for her own flight to be called. Even as she boarded the plane Mary Ellen was still worrying if she'd remembered to pack everything.

If she didn't, it was too late now, she philosophically decided. She was lucky to be boarding the plane at all. Apparently the airlines had overbooked, so Mary Ellen had been bumped up from economy and given a seat in the ritzier business-class section. The seat next to hers remained empty until the last moment, when a good-looking man in his early forties claimed the vacancy, and Mary Ellen's attention.

He was elegantly dressed in a business suit and had a touch of gray in his dark hair. He slid his leather briefcase beneath the seat ahead of him and cast an appreciative glance at Mary Ellen's legs.

Mary Ellen noted his action with an inner smile. She'd been undecided about what to wear on the plane—whether to dress for comfort or for looks. She was glad she opted for looks. The boost to her ego was worth every penny she'd spent on this outfit.

"Are you going to London on business or for pleasure?" he asked her, thereby initiating a conversation that continued throughout the eight-hour flight. Her traveling companion introduced himself as Philip Ramsey, a business executive on his way to a trade show in Frankfurt. Discovering that Mary Ellen and he would both be in Frankfurt on the same day, Philip immediately asked her out to dinner.

When Mary Ellen hesitated about accepting, he gave her his business card and wrote a number on the back of it. "This is where I can be reached in Frankfurt. Give me a call when you arrive and we'll confirm matters then."

Philip had a connecting flight to catch to Frankfurt, so he didn't have time to accompany Mary Ellen through customs. After she'd completed the formalities, she began searching for the promised Worldwind representative, to no avail. When she approached the airline's information desk and made an inquiry, she was addressed by another woman standing in line.

"You're waiting for Worldwind Tours too? So am I," the woman announced. "And the airline people don't have a clue where our guide is. They just told me to keep waiting, while they check into it."

Mary Ellen decided to do her waiting in a less congested area. The move didn't prevent her foot from almost being run over by an out-of-control luggage cart.

"Oh, I'm sorry!" her fellow Worldwind tour member apologized. "These things are hard to steer, aren't they? Since we're both waiting for Worldwind, we might as well wait together. My name is Mitzi Renaldo, by the way. Is this your first trip with Worldwind?"

Mary Ellen nodded. "It's also my first trip to Europe."

"Mine too," Mitzi admitted. "Just to be on the safe side I brought along my own guidebook. I don't intend to be completely dependent on our guide."

Mitzi's announcement was interrupted by the arrival of a Worldwind representative, who chastised them for waiting in the wrong place before bundling them and their luggage into a taxi. Mary Ellen barely had time to take note of the red double-decker buses passing by before the taxi took off with a startling lurch.

"My, this driving on the left-hand side takes some getting used to," Mitzi exclaimed as she braced herself in her seat.

You can say that again, Mary Ellen thought to herself as the taxi hurtled its way around a roundabout. *I hope I live long enough to reach London!*

Mitzi spent a great deal of the trip busily digging around in her oversize purse in search of her guidebook. She found it just as they reached one of London's more recognizable landmarks.

"Look!" Mitzi exclaimed, grabbing hold of Mary Ellen's arm in her excitement. "There's Buckingham Palace! Too bad our tour doesn't include a visit with the queen, huh?"

"I imagine she's pretty busy," Mary Ellen murmured. They were the only words she was able to insert before Mitzi went on another lengthy discourse about the next sight. Mary Ellen was soon worn out by Mitzi's avalanche of facts, and she welcomed their arrival at the hotel.

Mary Ellen had hoped to do some sightseeing right away, but the combination of jet lag and her shortage of sleep during the past few weeks finally caught up with her. After eating a light meal, she went to bed at an unfashionably early hour. Even more surprising she slept straight through to seven the next morning.

As predicted in *The Times* Mary Ellen had

picked up to read over breakfast, the weather in the British capital was partly sunny with showery spells. Her day passed in a rush of sightseeing activities and souvenir shopping before she set out to meet Jennifer for tea at the Ritz.

Her initial anticipation at the prospect of seeing Jennifer again was replaced by trepidation when she arrived at the famous hotel and joined the others who stood in line waiting to be seated. The opulent surroundings were intimidating. But no more so than the maître d' who turned his attention to the couple directly ahead of Mary Ellen.

"May I help you?" the formally dressed gentleman questioned the couple with a disapproving stare.

"Yes, we made a reservation for tea. The name is Dunright."

"I'm sorry, but we won't be able to seat you."

"Why not?"

"I'm afraid the gentleman's attire is too casual. We require a tie as well as a jacket." The maître d' sniffed his dismissal and moved on to Mary Ellen. "May I help you?"

Mary Ellen glanced down at her own attire with a worried frown. She was wearing a patterned silk blouse and a pair of elegantly tailored navy wool slacks. Her jacket belonged to her best raw silk suit and had a designer's label. But the maître d' was not impressed; she could read that much in his disdainful expression.

"I'm supposed to meet someone here for tea. Her last name is Ashford. Jennifer Ashford."

The maître d' took so long checking his list that Mary Ellen was certain she, too, was going to be turned away, just like the couple who'd been ahead of her. "Come this way," he finally instructed her.

"I thought I was going to get kicked out for sure," Mary Ellen confessed to Jennifer once she was seated. "Talk about disapproving. Whew!"

Jennifer didn't laugh, as Mary Ellen had expected her to. Now that Mary Ellen took a closer look at her friend, she realized that Jennifer looked pale and worried. "Is something wrong? It's not your father, is it?"

"No, Dad is recovering ahead of schedule."

"Then what is it?"

"I'm worried about Ty."

The sound of his name was enough to make Mary Ellen stiffen.

"I haven't heard from him since he returned to Europe," Jennifer continued, "and I'm afraid he might be in trouble."

"Ty's always in trouble," Mary Ellen retorted, "and he always manages to get himself out again. Don't waste your time worrying about him."

"He's my brother, of course I worry about him."

"I realize that, and I didn't mean to sound harsh, but he's an adult who can take care of himself. Let's not talk about him anymore. It still hurts me and I want to enjoy my vacation. Here I am, in Europe, and I intend to make the most of it! Who knows, I might even meet a charming man over here and fall for him, the way you did. How is Ian doing, anyway?"

"Fine."

"I'm glad. Now, stop looking so worried."

"I will, if you'll promise one thing."

Mary Ellen looked decidedly cautious. "What?"

"If you should happen to run into Ty, would you tell him to contact me?"

"Jennifer, Europe is a huge place. There's little chance that I'll run into Ty." Mary Ellen recited the assurance as if it were a good-luck charm.

"I know, but if you should—"

"I'll give him the message," Mary Ellen hurriedly agreed, confident that the occasion would not arise. "Now can we talk about something else? How about my first impressions of England?" The enthusiasm returned to her voice. "It's everything I thought it would be, and more. I'm glad I came." As their waiter served the scones they'd ordered, Mary Ellen went on to discuss the various tourist sites she'd visited and some of the people in her tour group. "Aside from the lady who constantly reads aloud from her guidebook, I've only spoken to the Fishbeins, a retired couple from Kalamazoo. The other people seem to be nice too."

"Where does your tour go from here?" Jennifer asked.

"We fly to Copenhagen in the morning."

"Copenhagen is a lovely city. You'll like it."

Jennifer was absolutely correct. Mary Ellen did like Copenhagen, at least what she saw of it through the bus window. Her first impressions were of a red-brick city bright with green copper roofs.

As soon as everyone's luggage was unloaded at the hotel, the group was herded into another bus and given a city tour of Copenhagen. Their first stop was the Amalienborg Palace, the queen of Denmark's residence, where they were just in time to watch the changing of the guard at noon.

"This makes up for missing the changing of the guard in London, doesn't it?" Irma Fishbein exclaimed in an enthralled voice.

"Sure does," her husband Sheldon agreed as he took some pictures. "Look at those bearskin hats, aren't they something?"

"It says here in my guidebook that Denmark is one of the oldest kingdoms in the world," Mitzi informed them.

Mary Ellen's attention was directed to focusing her camera on the colorful procession passing in front of her, so she didn't notice the man who was making his way through the crowd; closing in on her with the efficiency of a bloodhound. She had no knowledge of his presence until he'd reached her side and spoken to her.

"It's been a long time, Marielle," said Ty.

CHAPTER FOUR

Mary Ellen dropped her camera from fingers that had suddenly become all thumbs. Only the camera strap around her neck saved the photographic equipment from certain destruction. "What are *you* doing here?" The words came out midway between a wail and a curse.

"Did you miss me?" Ty actually had the gall to place an amorous arm around her shoulder.

Furious at his behavior she didn't even register the magic of his touch. "Go away!" she hissed, trying to shake off his arm. When that proved to be an impossible task, she began muttering under her breath. "You're not supposed to be here! Europe is a huge place, they said. Hah!"

"This is a public square, Marielle. I've got as

much right to be here as you do." He reached out to smooth away the tendrils of hair that her angry tirade had sent tumbling into her eyes.

She slapped away his caressing hand.

Their altercation was being observed by more than one pair of interested eyes. Ty noticed the attention of one man in particular, a good-looking Scandinavian who was looking at Mary Ellen with proprietary interest. "Do you know that guy?" Ty demanded.

Confused by the abrupt change of subject she said, "What guy?"

"The one who's looking at you and glaring at me."

"Oh, you mean that tall, blond, very attractive man?" she asked, deliberately intensifying Ty's displeasure. "That's Christian." She didn't add that he was the group's tour guide. "And he's not going to like it if you keep bothering me, so you'd better leave me alone. But before you go, there's one more thing I have to say."

Ty leaned closer as if they were sharing the most intimate of verbal exchanges. "And what's that, Marielle?"

Mary Ellen's expressive blue eyes glared their resentment at his cavalier attitude. "Call your sister. Jennifer is worried sick about you. She thinks you're in some kind of trouble."

"I am in trouble," he freely admitted.

Mary Ellen was tempted to ask him to elaborate, but she steeled herself against the momentary weakness. She'd been taken in by him before and had learned her lesson. "That's your problem. It has nothing to do with me."

"Oh, but you see, it does have a great deal to do with you, because *you're* going to help me get out of trouble."

"You must be crazy!"

"Not at all. I've given this plan a great deal of thought."

"Too bad. You forgot to figure in one important fact, and that is that I don't want anything to do with you. I have no intention of letting you ruin this vacation for me. I came to Europe to have a good time," she added with a deliberately inviting smile in Christian's direction.

The flirtatious gesture did not escape Ty's attention. "What kind of a good time?" he demanded suspiciously.

"Suffice it to say that having you along would cramp my style, Ty."

He looked thunderstruck. "You're planning on having a fling?"

"I prefer to call it a romantic encounter." She took advantage of his momentary shock and finally freed herself from his encircling arm.

Ty recovered quickly, recapturing her with his eyes if not his arms. "Whatever you want to call it, you can just forget about it."

"Oh?" Mary Ellen was regaining her confidence. "And why's that?"

"Because I have no intention of allowing you to do such a thing."

"How do you propose to stop me?"

"By joining your bus tour and keeping an eye on you."

Well aware that tour members had to prebook in the United States, she was not intimidated by his words. "Go ahead and try," she dared him.

"I will, Marielle. I will." Ty gave her one final smoldering look before he melted back into the crowd.

"Are you all right, Mary Ellen?" Christian asked, having finally reached her side. "I hope you were not being disturbed by that man."

"No problem," she reassured him. Taking a deep breath she added, "I'm fine."

Of course she wasn't fine; who would be, after meeting the one person on the face of the earth that you'd wanted to avoid at all costs? How had Ty known where to find her? Mary Ellen found it hard to believe that he just happened to be sightseeing at the Amalienborg Palace and wanted to say hi. He'd said something about being in trouble. Was he telling the truth or was that simply another line he was stringing? Why should she care?

You don't care, she told herself.

Then why was her breathing still erratic and her pulse racing?

Anger, that's why.

Christian's voice interrupted her intense self-discussion. "If you're ready, we'll return to the bus now."

It wasn't until Mary Ellen was boarding the bus that she realized she hadn't taken any photographs of the changing of the guard or of the square itself. Surrounded by the four symmetrical wings of the rococo palace, the square was one of the most beautiful in Europe. Christian had told them so before they'd gotten off the bus. Now, thanks to Ty, she'd missed recording it on film.

"Who was that good-looking man you were speaking to?" Irma asked Mary Ellen from her seat across the aisle.

"He was asking for directions."

"Were you able to help him?"

"I told him I couldn't help him." To which Mary Ellen silently added, *I should have told him where to go.*

She still found it hard to believe that Ty actually had the nerve to approach her and think he could enlist her help in whatever madcap scheme he'd gotten himself involved in this time. Did he think he could just drop her and pick her up again at will? She hadn't heard one word from him since he'd left Chicago so abruptly last month, just as she hadn't heard from him when he'd left Chicago seven years ago to join the Grand Prix circuit in Europe.

Obviously in his world people came and went as they pleased, no ties, no thought of tomorrow. Well, that might suit him just fine, but she wanted no part of it. If he knew what was good for him, Ty had better steer clear of her in future or he'd be in big trouble.

He's already in trouble, she reminded herself. Not that it seemed to have any adverse affect on him. Quite the opposite, in fact. He looked even better than he had in Chicago. The lines of strain around his mouth had diminished, and the reckless gleam in his brown eyes had grown brighter.

Upset with herself for noticing so much about him, Mary Ellen deliberately banished Ty from her thoughts and concentrated on what Christian was saying over the tour bus's loudspeaker system.

"The large cathedral we are now passing is the Marble Church, or as we Danes call it, the Marmorkirke. Construction had to be abandoned when marble became too expensive, and the building lay uncompleted for more than a century until a banker came up with the necessary funds. The church was finally completed in 1894, a tribute to Danish tenacity."

Mary Ellen took a photograph of the church through the bus window, but her thoughts bounced back to Ty, spurred by Christian's use of the word *tenacity*. It was a word applicable to Ty when he wanted something. She could only hope that he would give up the ridiculous idea of joining her on the bus tour.

As soon as they reached their next destination, the bus stopped and everyone dutifully got off. Christian waited until the group had gathered around him before he began speaking. "We are standing in front of the Gefion Fountain. The bronze figures of a goddess driving four oxen commemorate the legend of Gefion, to whom the king of Sweden offered all the land she could plow out of his country in one night. So she turned her four sons into oxen . . ."

"No maternal instincts, I guess," Irma murmured in an aside to Mary Ellen.

". . . and plowed away the island of Zealand, on which the city of Copenhagen is located. Now, for those of you who would like a walk, the Langelinie is a half-mile promenade through the park and along the waterfront. You will have a twenty-minute break to take pictures and enjoy the walk. Those of you who would prefer to ride in the bus may come with me. We will all meet up at the statue of Hans Christian Andersen's Little Mermaid, the symbol of Copenhagen." Christian had already taught them the correct pronunciation of the city, which was *Copen-hay-gen.* "Remember, twenty minutes. Please, don't be late. We still have a lot to see yet."

"Are you going to walk or ride in the bus?" Irma asked Mary Ellen.

"Walk," she replied. "It's a nice day and I could use the fresh air."

Irma diplomatically restrained herself from pointing out that they'd all been out in the fresh air a mere ten minutes ago when they'd stopped to watch the changing of the guard. "Sheldon and I are going to walk too. How about you, Viola?"

The forty-year-old school teacher from Australia grinned before replying, "After all the

71

food I've been eating, I think I'd better walk some of it off."

"I don't think you need to lose any weight, Viola. You're fine just as you are." Irma turned to the man standing next to her. "I'm sure Hank agrees with me."

Hank Denton, divorced with a thirteen-year-old son named Archie, was the only unattached male on the tour, and Irma obviously felt it was her duty to match him up with Viola. Mary Ellen was relieved that so far Irma's heavy-handed matchmaking had been confined to those two members of the tour. She'd hate to have Irma playing Cupid for her.

"It says here in my guidebook that *Langelinie* means 'long line,'" Mitzi announced.

Everyone hurried off on their walk before Mitzi launched into any more detailed trivia.

Mary Ellen broke away from the rest of the group to take pictures, determined to make up for her lapse at the Amalienborg Palace. And so it was that once again, Ty was able to approach her without warning. He simply materialized in front of her camera lens, just as she pressed the shutter.

"You again!"

"We've got to stop meeting like this," he quipped with an irreverent grin.

"I agree completely." Mary Ellen was not amused. "Go away."

"Don't you want to hear what I've got planned?"

"No."

"All right. But remember, I did offer to tell you, so don't get upset after the deed is done."

"I'll be far more upset if you don't leave me alone this instant." She glared at him. "I mean it, Ty."

"Okay." He shrugged with mocking acquiescence. "If that's the way you want it."

"It is."

"Enjoy your walk, Marielle. And pay special attention to the Little Mermaid. It's always reminded me a bit of you."

As before, Ty simply melted back into the group of pedestrians enjoying the fine day.

Throughout the rest of the day's tour Mary Ellen kept expecting Ty to show up again. She tried to concentrate on what Christian was telling them. She remembered some things, such as his saying that Copenhagen has a fondness for playful buildings. The fact that the Stock Exchange has a spire of entwining dragon tails also stuck in her mind. Unfortunately the rest of Christian's presentation went in one ear and out the other.

The blame did not lie with Christian; he was an excellent tour guide. Nor was Mary Ellen bored or inattentive. Quite simply, the strain of having to keep a sharp lookout for Ty was taking its toll on her.

By the time the tour returned to the hotel, Mary Ellen was a nervous wreck. Thinking an apéritif might calm her nerves she accepted an invitation from the Fishbeins for a drink in the hotel bar. They were joined by Mitzi and Viola.

73

Sheldon was delighted to be the lone male at their table. "Ah, this is the life. A whiskey in my hand and a bevy of beauties by my side."

"Now, you behave yourself, you sweet-talker, you." Irma gave Sheldon a teasing slap on his hand.

The incident reminded Mary Ellen of how she'd slapped away Ty's hand earlier that day, and she glanced around, half expecting him to appear out of nowhere again.

Viola shared some amusing anecdotes about her students back in Sydney, and Mitzi even abandoned her guidebook for once to relate several entertaining stories of her own. Despite the lively conversation Mary Ellen still had a hard time concentrating. *That drink must have zonked me more than I expected,* she decided.

Under the circumstances Mary Ellen elected to make an early night of it and made her apologies to the others.

"You do look tired," Irma noted. "Poor thing, you're probably not over your jet lag yet. Sheldon and I have traveled so much that we don't even get jet lag anymore. We're going out dancing tonight at a nightclub we heard about."

"Have fun," Mary Ellen replied, envying the retired couple's stamina.

"We will."

Riding the elevator to her thirteenth-floor room Mary Ellen grimaced at the number displayed on her room key—1313. At the moment her need for a safe haven away from the threat of Ty's presence overrode whatever superstitious misgivings she might have had.

As soon as she got to her room she planned on placing a long-distance call to Jennifer in England, telling her that Ty was alive and as impossible as ever. Her intended phone call was forgotten when she walked into her room and found an unexpected surprise sprawled out on her bed—Ty!

He met her stunned look with a devilish grin. "Welcome home, roomie."

"Off! Get off my bed! This minute!" Her words may have been incoherent, but her dismay was crystal clear.

"*Our* bed, Marielle," Ty mockingly corrected her.

"How did you get in here?"

"With my key."

"*Your* key?" she repeated in amazement.

"That's right." He held it out for her perusal. "You see, when I explained everything to the Worldwind people, they were very helpful— bent the rules a bit and allowed me to join your tour."

"No." Mary Ellen sank onto the room's only chair—fortuitously placed nearby, because her shaky legs weren't capable of supporting her any longer. "What did you tell them?"

"That we had a lover's spat—all the world loves a lover, you know—and I had to do something to put the kibosh on your idiotic plan to have an affair. This way I'll be able to keep an eye on you."

"You said you were in trouble," she reminded him. "I'm sure you've got better things to do than keep an eye on me."

"As it so happens, my joining you on the bus tour is the perfect solution for both problems. For reasons I'd rather not go into at the moment, I've got to lie low for a while. What better place for me to hide than in a busload of tourists? Who would think to look for me there?"

"No one. Because you're not going to be in a busload of tourists. At least, not this busload of tourists. I won't have it."

"Why, Marielle, if I didn't know better I'd say you were trying to avoid me."

"I am trying to avoid you. I wish I were doing a better job of it," she added in a muttered undertone.

Even her attempts at giving Ty the evil eye backfired and turned into a reluctant appraisal. He'd removed the battered brown leather bomber jacket he'd been wearing when he'd first accosted her, the one that made him look like Indiana Jones. Actually the resemblance was due as much to the daring self-confidence the two men shared as to any similarity in their attire.

Ty was now wearing a simple blue shirt and a pair of dark slacks that emphasized the athletic leanness of his body. His dark hair was rumpled, but it was the self-satisfaction in his brown eyes that brought her to her senses. He thought he had it made. Her gaze narrowed in on the piece of metal he held in his hand.

"Give me that key," she demanded. Not waiting for him to comply with her order, she reached over and tried forcibly to take it from his hand.

In a flash Ty had tugged her onto the bed and rolled on top of her, thereby pinning her to the bedspread. "Shame on you, Marielle. Didn't your mother ever teach you not to grab?"

"I know your mother taught you not to grab, but that doesn't seem to be stopping you," she observed caustically.

"Why, Marielle, I'm only trying to protect myself. The same way you're trying to protect yourself from me. There's really no need to." There was a hint of reproach in his voice. "I'm not going to hurt you."

"That's right. You're not going to hurt me because you're not going to be anywhere near me. You're leaving this minute! Do you hear me?"

"Half the people on this floor can probably hear you, Marielle. Shhhhh . . ."

"Don't shush me!" She was furious.

"Okay, I'll kiss you instead."

His lips were almost touching hers at that point anyway. It was a simple matter for him to erase the remaining distance between them. He did so with efficiency, capturing her protest and muffling it against her mouth.

Mary Ellen knew perfectly well what she

should do. She should fight him, and she did—for about one minute. She would have been able to hold out longer had he not searched out and found her erogenous zones as only he knew how to. Unable to resist the changing tide of her own emotions, she stopped listening to logic and did what she wanted. She returned his kisses, her hunger matching his.

CHAPTER FIVE

Mary Ellen's response not only surprised her, it surprised Ty as well. Contrary to what Mary Ellen might think, he wasn't as sure of her as he pretended to be. Hell, he wasn't sure of her at all.

He knew he had no right to expect her help or her understanding. But, by God, he needed her. His kiss reflected that hungry desperation.

He found her mouth warm, sweet, and very vulnerable to the touch of his tongue. Drawing her closer Ty capitalized on the sensuous discovery. Mary Ellen moaned in pleasure as she joined in the evocative give and take, the gliding thrusts of their tongues mimicking the pagan rhythm of total possession.

Daring further intimacies Ty lowered his

body so that he was now resting atop her. They fit together with erotic precision, his hardness conforming to her softness. His knee nudged her legs apart and he moved against her, letting her feel the strength of his arousal.

The contact was electrifying. Ty's hands and lips joined forces to intensify her excitement until she reached a state of mindless rapture. Her eyes closed and her grasp on reality faded. It took her more than a moment to realize that the pounding she was hearing wasn't her own heartbeat or Ty's. The loud noise was coming from the door to her hotel room.

"Mary Ellen? Are you all right? It's Christian."

"Tell him to get lost," Ty muttered as his tongue took another swipe at her earlobe.

"I'll be right there, Christian," she called out. She slipped from Ty's grasp with an agility born out of acute embarrassment. Frantically looking around the room she grabbed Ty's coat and him, hoping to stash both somewhere out of sight. "The bathroom," she whispered. "Go hide in the bathroom."

"Why?"

"Don't ask questions, just do it." She was nudging him backward even as she spoke, until he was on the other side of the bathroom door. "Now, stay in there. I'll be right back."

Mary Ellen closed the bathroom door and reached for the door to her room, opening it a mere crack. "I was resting, Christian. Is something wrong?"

"I just got word from the central office that a friend of yours has joined our tour. A Mr. Tyler Stevenson. Since such a late arrival is rather an unusual occurrence, I wanted to make sure everything is in order. This man really is a friend of yours, yes?"

"Uh, yes." Mary Ellen shot a nervous glance over to the closed bathroom door before opening her room door several more inches. "We go way back."

"I see. Then you have no objections to him sharing accommodations with you?"

"Sharing. . . ." Mary Ellen's voice trailed away. "Is that really necessary?"

Before Christian could reply, the bathroom door opened and Ty stood there, dressed in nothing but a skimpy bath towel! "The tub's all yours, honey." He dropped a kiss to her startled lips and placed a possessive arm around her shoulder. "Hi, I'm Ty Stevenson." He held out a hand to Christian with man-to-man candor. "You must be the terrific tour guide Mary Ellen's been telling me about. How can we help you?"

"I wanted to confirm that the unusual circumstances of your late arrival met with Mary Ellen's approval," Christian stated.

Ty nodded his own approval. "I appreciate that. It's reassuring to know that you've been looking out for Mary Ellen." He leaned forward in a confidential manner. "I'm sure you know how some men will try and take advantage of innocent young women traveling

81

abroad for the first time." He shook his head as if offended by such behavior. "That's why I decided to forget our little lover's quarrel and fly right over here to take care of Mary Ellen myself. So you see, there's nothing to be concerned about. We're just fine. Mary Ellen and I both appreciate you checking on things, though. Thanks for stopping by." Ty gave Christian a cheerful wave before closing the door.

Mary Ellen hadn't stamped her foot in anger since she was seven, but she did so now, narrowly missing squashing Ty's bare feet with the sole of her walking shoes. "Talk about unmitigated gall!"

"Marielle, the poor man was only doing his job."

"I wasn't talking about Christian, I'm talking about you!"

"I guess you're pretty upset, huh?"

"That's putting it mildly."

"Okay, look, let's sit down and talk this over. I realize I owe you an explanation."

"Get dressed first." Her request held a certain amount of impatient desperation. "I can't concentrate while you're traipsing around half nude."

Ty grinned. The gleam in his dark eyes was nothing short of devilish. "Bothers you, does it?"

Mary Ellen glared at his bare chest. Did he have to be so attractive?

"Don't do that." He smoothed a finger across her forehead. "You'll get wrinkles."

"I'll get gray hair if I have to wait around much longer for your explanation," she muttered. "Get dressed."

Instead of returning to the bathroom where he'd left his clothes, Ty headed for the built-in closet. He opened it and Mary Ellen saw his clothes hanging next to hers.

"Pretty sure of yourself, aren't you?" she said bitterly.

"Not at all," he replied in a quiet voice.

Mary Ellen walked over to the window and stood gazing out at the uninspiring view of the hotel's inner courtyard. "I may be willing to help you out of whatever trouble you've gotten yourself into," she distantly informed him. "But there are two conditions. The first is that you tell me exactly what kind of trouble you're in."

"And the second?" The sound of Ty fastening his jeans punctuated his question.

"We'll get to that after you've complied with the first condition." She heard the rustle of cotton as he pulled on a clean shirt. Turning to face him she demanded the truth. "Tell me right now what's going on."

"I've upset a gambling companion, and I'm persona non grata in his books right now."

Visions of enormous gambling debts filled her head. "How much did you lose?" She was almost afraid to ask.

"Actually I didn't lose. I won."

83

Her concern turned into confusion. "I don't understand."

"I suppose I'd better begin at the beginning."

"That's usually a good idea."

"Shall we sit down?"

"I prefer to stand, thank you." She had no intention of getting waylaid on that bed again.

Unable to put off the inevitable any longer Ty began speaking. "I left Chicago so abruptly last month because of an urgent phone call I received from a very good friend of mine."

"What's her name?" Mary Ellen taunted.

Ty gave her a reprimanding look. *"His* name is Lars Nielsen, and he lives here in Copenhagen. He's been on the racing circuit about as long as I have, and he's helped me out of more than one tight spot. He called me because this time he needed my help. He'd lost a large amount of money in Monte Carlo, more than he could afford, and he had reason to believe that he'd been double-crossed. Knowing my special skill with cards Lars asked me to help recover the money for him." Ty paused to see how Marielle was receiving his story so far. Unfortunately he couldn't see her eyes, because she was studying the pattern on the rug with infuriating intensity.

Mary Ellen was trying to assimilate what he'd told her. Ty was a skilled gambler. Since when? Wait a minute, what about that game of strip poker he'd talked her into playing during their summer-long affair? She'd teasingly accused him of cheating . . .

Disconcerted by her silence Ty continued. "I didn't think it would take me longer than a few days at most to take care of things, and then I thought I'd fly back to Chicago. But I underestimated the complexity of the situation, and by then it was too late to call you. I knew you'd hang up on me before I could explain, and you would probably have torn up any letter I wrote you. I knew you were coming to Europe in April, so I figured it would be easier for me to get in touch with you over here."

"Go on."

Ty ran an impatient hand through his hair. Couldn't she say something more encouraging? "As I said, things were more complicated than I expected. It took me several weeks to gain the con man's confidence and be invited to sit in on a poker game. I did win Lars's money back for him. The problem is that the cardsharp, who calls himself Mr. Q, thinks that I was cheating."

"Were you?"

"Of course," Ty freely admitted. "But then, so was Mr. Q. And the only way I could win was to beat him at his own game. I did, but Mr. Q is a poor loser. You might say he's rather peeved with me at the moment. He's having me followed." Ty omitted saying that the two men following him could hardly find their way out of a paper bag. Instead he waited for Mary Ellen's reaction. She looked at him, really looked at him, and he saw worry in her eyes. Worry and concern for him.

"Followed? Why? Does Mr. Q want the money back?"

"I already returned the money to Lars, so I don't think I'm being followed for that reason."

"Then why?"

"Mr. Q wants to teach me a lesson."

Mary Ellen was horrified. "You mean that these men are thugs hired to beat you up or worse?"

Ty paused, as if reluctant to say anything further. Actually he was congratulating himself on doing his research on Mr. Q ahead of time. For all his recklessness Ty wasn't stupid, and he didn't have a death wish. So he'd carefully checked out the man he would be fleecing. Mr. Q was only a small-time dealer who'd already made the mistake of getting greedy and stepping on a number of big leaguers' toes. Speculation was that Mr. Q's days were numbered, probably with single digits. Had Ty thought he was really in any serious danger he would never have gotten Mary Ellen involved.

As it was, he saw no reason not to make the most of his situation in order to stay with Mary Ellen. Deciding that a touch of noble martyrdom might be in order, he made a heroic speech instead of answering her question. "I don't want you to feel obligated to help me. If you really feel it's too much to ask, I'll understand."

"Of course it's not too much to ask," Mary

Ellen automatically denied before she realized that she still didn't know exactly what Ty had planned. "Er, what exactly *are* you asking?"

"Obviously Mr. Q isn't ready yet to let bygones be bygones, so I figured I'd lie low for a while until the storm blows over. As I said before, no one would think to look for me in a busload of tourists. It's not exactly my normal style. So I thought I'd accompany you on your trip. What do you say?"

Mary Ellen was worried about Ty's safety, but she couldn't help being suspicious of his motives in choosing this method of concealment. To protect herself she brought up condition number two.

"I'll help you, but I won't go to bed with you," she stated bluntly. "I'll share my room with you, but not my bed."

Amusement glinted in his eyes. "In case you hadn't noticed, there's only one bed in this room."

"Actually it's a pair of twin beds pushed together. We'll just push them apart."

His amusement faded as he realized that she was serious. "What about other rooms? We won't be staying in Copenhagen forever."

"I realize that. We'll have to manage, but not in the same bed."

Ty was not pleased by this turn of events, but he was confident in his ability to make Mary Ellen change her mind. He had to be, it was all he had to go on. That and her passionate, if unwilling, response to his kiss.

"So? Do you agree?" she asked him.

"I agree not to make love to you until you ask me to," he compromised. "However I feel it only fair to warn you that I intend doing everything in my power to make sure you do ask me, and soon!"

Mary Ellen shrugged and raised her chin in a gesture Ty recognized. "Forewarned is forearmed."

Another knock on the door cut into Ty's reply.

"Who is it?" Mary Ellen called out.

"Room service," an unfamiliar voice replied.

"What are you doing?" she demanded as Ty headed for the door.

"I'm going to open the door."

She grabbed his arm. "Don't do that. It could be a trap! I didn't order room service."

"No, but I did." Ty dropped a reassuring kiss to her lips before opening the door.

Mary Ellen kept staring at the hotel employee, trying to discern any sign of devious behavior. The man didn't look threatening, but it was hard to tell. She stiffened when he adjusted the steak knives beside the place setting. Now he was reaching for another sharp instrument, the corkscrew for the wine. She followed his every move. Were his fingers trembling? Her eyes narrowed. He poured the wine, spilling some in the process, then beat a hasty retreat.

"Marielle, you were watching that poor waiter like a hawk."

"Did you notice that his hands were shaking and that he couldn't wait to get out of here?"

"That's because you were staring holes through him," Ty said with an exasperated sigh. "Look, let me worry about security. You come over here and sit down. You must be hungry after a hard day of sightseeing."

Once she began eating Mary Ellen realized how hungry she was. Ty had ordered two steak dinners with potatoes and vegetables. She barely touched her glass of red wine, but she did clean her plate.

"What did you think of the Little Mermaid?" Ty asked her as they ate their fresh fruit salad for dessert.

"It was nice."

"Did you hear the story behind the statue?"

"What story?"

"Legend has it that the sculptor and the model for the statue were lovers. That's why he was able to capture her wistful expression so well. He told her to think about the way they'd made love the night before."

She gave him a look filled with long-suffering resignation. "Only you could turn the character from a Hans Christian Andersen fairy tale into a sex object."

"Hey, I'm not the only one. I'll have you know that a number of sailors believe that kissing the mermaid brings good fortune."

Mary Ellen remained skeptical. "I'm sure that isn't in the guidebooks. Mitzi would have told us if it had been."

"Who's Mitzi? I thought Christian was the tour guide."

"He is. Mitzi is a tour member who is an expert on guidebooks. You'll meet her and the others tomorrow." Mary Ellen sighed. "I can imagine what Irma will say when she sees you. She'll give you the third degree for sure."

"All I'll tell her is my name, rank, and serial number," Ty solemnly assured her.

"I meant to ask you earlier—isn't it dangerous to use your real name while you're on the bus trip?"

"I'm clean out of fake passports."

"Oh, I hadn't thought of that. Of course you'll need to show a passport when we leave the country."

"Speaking of which, when are we leaving Copenhagen?"

"The day after tomorrow." She paused to spear the cherry from her fruit salad, which she'd been saving for her last bite. "We'll be taking a ferry down to Germany."

"What's on the agenda for tomorrow?"

"I'm going on an optional castle tour."

"If you're going, so am I."

"Wouldn't it be safer for you to stay here in the room?"

"Safer for whom?" he demanded.

"What's that supposed to mean?"

"It means that I haven't forgotten the way you looked at Christian. I thought we'd already established the fact that any ideas you might have in the romance department had better include me."

Mary Ellen calmly got up, walked over to the telephone, and handed the receiver to Ty. "Call your sister. And just for the record, if you weren't already in trouble, I'd be very tempted to cause you some bodily harm myself."

"Marielle, my body is always at your disposal, you know that." The words were seductively wrapped up in that husky voice of his. He studied her mouth with hungry intent even as he spoke into the phone. "Yes, operator, I'd like to make a long distance call to England. . . ."

Difficult though it was, Mary Ellen did manage to break free of Ty's spell. A long shower sounded like a good cure for her increasing case of restlessness, so she gathered up her things and stepped into the bathroom, making sure to lock the door after her. When she finally stepped out again she thought she'd gotten her emotions back under control, but that was before she saw Ty's sleeping attire.

Catching her staring at him Ty looked down and grinned. "You like?"

Mary Ellen lifted her chin and gave him a haughty stare.

He was not intimidated. "You seemed upset by my earlier state of undress, so I called the front desk and asked if there was some place I could purchase a pair of pajamas. Quick as a wink a bellboy was dispatched to do the job, and *voilà!*" Ty snapped his fingers. "They don't fit too badly, do they?"

The only thing bad was what he was doing to her blood pressure! The dark-blue material clung to his lean thighs, the drawstring waistband riding low on his hips. His chest was bare. Mary Ellen swallowed, wetting a throat that had suddenly gone dry. "I thought pajamas were sold with both tops and bottoms."

"They are, but I thought the top would look better on you." Ty held up the dark-blue silk pajama top for her appraisal.

She shook her head and tightened the belt on her nylon robe. "I've already got a nightgown, thank you."

"I know, but this matches your eyes."

It might match her eyes, but it also matched his pajama bottoms, and she had no intention of being one half of a pair. "You haven't moved the beds apart yet."

Ty made no comment on her abrupt change of subject. "I was just about to do that when you came out of the bathroom."

Mary Ellen doubted that was true, but she kept her thoughts to herself as Ty shifted the furniture.

"Farther," she said. "Move the bed farther away."

"Marielle, if I move this bed any farther it'll be hanging out of the window. Relax. I'm not going to pounce on you. I'll give you ample warning before I launch any seductive attacks, okay?"

"I'd prefer that you not launch any seductive attacks period."

"How about a cease-fire for the night?" he suggested. "Both sides can resume their positions tomorrow, but for now, what do you say that we both try and get a good night's sleep. I don't know about you, but I've had a long day."

By the time Ty was finished in the bathroom Mary Ellen had already turned off her bedside light and had pulled the blankets up to her chin. Surprisingly she was able to fall asleep without much trouble. She even overslept the next morning, which meant that everyone else was already seated for breakfast when she walked into the hotel's dining room. Everyone, that is, except for Ty, who was still upstairs in her room making a phone call.

"Last night certainly was full of excitement, wasn't it?" Irma noted as Mary Ellen took her seat at the table they shared.

Mary Ellen almost choked on her orange juice. "I beg your pardon?"

Irma seemed puzzled by Mary Ellen's blushing stammer. "I was talking about the incident with Archie."

Mary Ellen almost sighed with relief. Irma hadn't been referring to Ty and his occupation of her room, but to Hank's young son. "I'm sorry, I misunderstood. What happened with Archie?"

"He disappeared last night. Everyone was out looking for him. Viola soon found him, though."

"Where was he?"

"Visiting Copenhagen's red-light district. No

harm was done, thank goodness. Viola caught up with him before he'd ventured very far."

"What made her think to look for him there?" Mary Ellen asked. After all, Archie was only thirteen.

"Well, you know that Viola sits across from Archie and his father on the bus. When the city tour drove through the red-light district as part of our tour, she happened to notice the rapt expression on Archie's face. And you know how Archie is, I don't think much gets past that Sony Walkman he's constantly listening to."

Mary Ellen was actually indebted to Archie for keeping the limelight away from herself. Ty joined her for breakfast, but his presence didn't raise any eyebrows until he boarded the bus with her and took the heretofore empty seat beside her.

Aware of everyone's eyes on them Mary Ellen doggedly turned her face toward the window as the bus slowly pulled into traffic.

Ty was undeterred by her withdrawal. He simply leaned across and joined her in looking out the window. "What's so interesting out there, or are you just trying to ignore me again?"

Ignore him? How could she when she could feel his warm breath on her cheek, his body pressed against hers? His mere presence demanded attention.

Ty's presence on the bus also caught the attention of two men who were standing on the street corner, waiting for the light to change.

The short stocky man with the slicked-down hair grabbed the arm of his gangling companion. "Look, Josef, there he is! We finally got lucky. I told you we'd find him if we kept looking."

"What's he doing on a tour bus?"

"That's what we have to find out. Hurry, to the car. We must follow them!"

CHAPTER SIX

Unaware that they were being followed Ty and Mary Ellen continued their battle of wills as the bus headed out of Copenhagen and into the surrounding countryside.

"Would you stop that?" Mary Ellen whispered as Ty kissed her ear for the third time in as many minutes. "Everyone is looking at us."

Ty made a big show of straightening and checking the other passengers. "Actually they're all enjoying the scenery and not paying the least attention to us."

"That's what we should be doing, enjoying the scenery."

"Oh, I am, Marielle. I am." His attention remained focused on her as he reached out and fingered several strands of her hair.

She found herself grinning for no good reason. This wouldn't do at all. How was she supposed to maintain her distance at this rate? She carefully composed her expression.

"Too late, the damage has been done." He wagged his finger at her. "I saw that grin, it's no good trying to hide it now."

Her newfound composure crumbled. "You're impossible, do you know that?"

"I pride myself on it," he declared.

After a morning spent touring Frederiksborg Castle, Denmark's National Historical Museum, everyone was looking forward to sitting down and enjoying an authentic Scandinavian smorgasbord. The meal was set out in the banquet room of a nearby hotel and was arranged exclusively for tour groups. A center table displayed a variety of traditional foods: smoked and pickled fish from Sweden, cheeses from Norway, and, from Denmark, *smørrebrød*, open-faced sandwiches artistically decorated with a creative variety of meat, fish, egg, and cheese.

Mary Ellen knew that Irma had practically been bursting with curiosity all morning, and the other woman finally got a chance to corner Mary Ellen.

"I don't mean to be prying, dear, but isn't the man you're sitting with the same man who approached you during the changing of the guard in Copenhagen?"

Mary Ellen nodded.

"But I thought you said he was only asking you for directions," Irma said.

Mary Ellen had never been good at telling lies, even white ones, so she decided to stick as close to the truth as she could from now on. "I wasn't expecting to see Ty there. You see, we'd had an argument. . . ."

"Say no more, I understand. The two of you knew each other before, right?"

Mary Ellen nodded.

"I suspected as much." Irma nodded her head sagaciously. "I hope you'll forgive me for saying this, but I didn't think you were the kind of girl who'd pick up a strange man in Copenhagen. I told Sheldon so."

Hearing his name mentioned Sheldon looked up from the salad he was serving himself. "Isn't this spread something?"

Eagerly accepting the change in subject Mary Ellen agreed. "It certainly is."

Archie joined them and looked at the food with dismay. "They don't have hamburgers?"

"Afraid not," Mary Ellen replied.

"Wanna try some pickled herring?" Sheldon asked Archie with a Machiavellian grin.

Archie's eyes widened and he hurriedly shook his head, stepping away from them as if worried that Sheldon might force-feed him.

"That wasn't very nice," Irma reprimanded her husband.

"It wasn't very nice of Archie to walk out last night and get lost either," Sheldon retorted.

Irma patted her husband's sleeve. "No real

harm was done. Let's let bygones be bygones, hmmm?"

The phrase reminded Mary Ellen of Ty's comment about Mr. Q, a man who was not about to let bygones be bygones. Her eyes automatically sought out Ty, who was already seated at their table, his plate laden with food. He and the normally untalkative Hank were deep in conversation. She had to admit that Ty seemed to have no trouble fitting right in with the group.

As they ate their lunch Mitzi looked up from her guidebook to say, "Did you know that Denmark's tallest mountain is shorter than the Eiffel Tower?"

"I'm looking forward to seeing the Eiffel Tower when we get to Paris," Mary Ellen stated, hoping to distract Mitzi before she launched a full-scale recitation of facts.

Undaunted, Mitzi continued. "The entire country of Denmark is one sixteenth the size of Texas."

"I wish I was in Texas," Archie muttered morosely as he stared down at the strange-looking food on his plate.

"Listen to this," Mitzi exclaimed. " 'Except for the Bible the stories of Hans Christian Andersen have been more widely translated and read than any other works of literature.' "

"That's strange," Viola noted, joining the conversation for the first time. "I would have thought that the works of Shakespeare held that honor."

Mitzi immediately became defensive. "Well, my guidebook says . . ."

"And we mustn't question Mitzi's guidebook," Ty whispered to Mary Ellen with an accompanying caress under the table.

She grabbed hold of his hand and placed it back on his knee. "We mustn't do that either!" she told him in an angry undertone. Her glare told him that he'd be in trouble if he tried it again.

She should have known that trouble had never dissuaded Ty. He did keep his hand on his own knee, but he also retained possession of her hand, which was now sandwiched between his warm palm and the warm denim of his jeans. She tugged, but he wouldn't let her go.

"Tell us about yourself, Ty," Irma invited as he and Mary Ellen silently hand-wrestled under the table.

"What would you like to know?" he returned with a deliberately expansive smile.

Mary Ellen got the message. She stopped struggling and started praying that Ty would remember his teasing promise only to reveal his name, rank, and serial number. She knew that he could turn the most innocent of situations into something outrageous. Case in point was the way his long fingers were caressing her hand under the table!

"How long have you and Mary Ellen known each other?" Irma asked.

"Oh, Marielle and I practically grew up together back in Chicago." Ty omitted adding that he no longer lived there. "You might say we were teenage sweethearts."

Mary Ellen gritted her teeth and pinched his knee.

Unaware of Ty's brief grimace Irma continued her questioning. "Is this your first trip to Europe, Ty?"

"No." Seeing the storm clouds gathering in Mary Ellen's expressive eyes, Ty finally released her hand. "This is my first bus tour, though. I'm looking forward to sharing the experience with Marielle."

Dream on, Mary Ellen thought to herself. *There's no way I'm sharing any more experiences with you, Tyler Stevenson!*

After lunch the group got back on the bus and they headed off for Elsinore. During the drive Christian used the bus's loudspeaker system to give them a thumbnail history of Denmark's royal family. "A thousand years ago there was a king of Denmark named Gorm the Old. His family has ruled here ever since. In the past their kingdom included Sweden and Norway. One of the kings, Svend Forkbeard, even conquered parts of England before William the Conqueror did. Svend was not the only early monarch with an extraordinary name. There was also a Harald Bluetooth, Magnus the Good, and Eric the Very Good."

Under cover of the tour members' laughter, Ty leaned close to whisper into Mary Ellen's ear. "What do you think I would have been called, had I been king then? Tyler the Exceptionally Good?"

"Tyler the Fork-Tongued," she returned.

His laughter caught her off balance. "Does it feel like I have a forked tongue?" he asked before curling his tongue into a tool of seduction and launching a surprise attack on a sensitive spot behind her ear.

Mary Ellen shivered with pleasure. Then she remembered the two-sided sword of such pleasure and she shifted away from him. "Feelings can be deceptive."

Ty sighed and told himself that Rome wasn't won in a day.

Christian had completed his speech on Denmark's history and proceeded on to a few specifics about their next destination. "Elsinore, or *Helsingør* as it's called in Danish, is famous for Kronborg Castle, better known as Hamlet's castle. Shakespeare's play was set here at Elsinore."

The castle, turreted and formidable, loomed over the narrow sound separating Denmark and Sweden.

"Come along, everyone," Christian told them when they arrived at Kronborg Castle, "we must hurry. The tour is about to begin. Follow me."

"I feel like a kindergartner playing follow-the-leader," Ty muttered.

Mary Ellen doubted that Ty had ever played follow-the-leader, even as a kindergartner.

He'd never been a follower; he was too independent, too stubborn, too much of a loner.

Her thoughts were interrupted by the castle's special guide, who was telling them that Shakespeare had never seen Elsinore, but had heard about it. "He also heard about the twelfth-century tale of Prince Amleth, whose story provided the basis for Hamlet," the guide added. "The castle, rumored to be the greatest in all of Europe, was built as a fortress to intimidate the passing ships into paying a toll for using this sound."

As they toured the castle, Mary Ellen experienced the eerie feeling that they were being followed. Her frequent glances over her shoulder were noticed by Ty.

He took her aside and asked, "Is something wrong?"

"I have a funny feeling, like we're being followed."

"We are, by the next tour group. Listen, you can hear them. It sounds like it's a French version of our tour."

"I guess you're right."

"I know I'm right."

Nevertheless Mary Ellen couldn't shake her uneasy feeling. She tuned out the rest of the guide's commentary and listened for the sound of the French voices they'd heard before. But she heard nothing.

"And that's the end of our tour. For those of you who are adventurous, I would recommend a visit down to the castle's cavernous dungeons."

"Now, that sounds like something up my alley," Ty said.

Mary Ellen shivered. "You go ahead, I'll wait up here for you."

The other members of their tour agreed with Mary Ellen. They preferred the beckoning interior of the castle's gift shop over the gloomy interior of a dungeon. So Ty was on his own in the exploration of the dungeons.

Elsewhere in the castle two other men were also discussing the dungeons. "Are you certain he is coming this way?" Josef asked his partner, Pierre, as they both waited in said dungeon for Ty's appearance. They had been following him throughout the castle. Ambushing Ty in the dungeon had been Pierre's idea.

"I heard him tell the woman he wanted to see the dungeons," Pierre replied. "Quickly, take care of those light bulbs. We want it to be dark in here when he walks in. Then you can grab him. You will see, this will be the easiest twenty thousand dollars we've ever earned!"

"Are you sure you won't join me?" Ty asked Mary Ellen. "This is your last chance."

"No, thank you. I need to buy some film, so I'll wait for you by the gift shop." Disturbed by her continuing sense of something being wrong, she asked, "Are you sure you should go down to the dungeons by yourself? After all, you did say that someone is trailing you. . . ."

"And they haven't found me; they don't even know where to look. I'm a big boy, Marielle, I can take care of myself."

"If that were true you wouldn't be standing next to me on this bus tour," she retorted.

"Touché," he wryly acknowledged. "But I'm perfectly safe here at Elsinore. Go get your film, I'll be back before you know it."

"Shouldn't he have been down here by now?" Josef asked in a complaining voice. "I don't like it here in the dark."

"Quiet!" Pierre hissed. "Someone is coming. Get ready!"

Mary Ellen's paranoia increased the moment Ty was gone. She quickly bought her film and left the gift shop, not even bothering to look at the selection of Hamlet souvenirs. She'd forgotten to wear her watch, so she had no idea of the actual length of Ty's absence, but it felt like it had been long enough to tour several dungeons. Surely he should be coming back any moment now?

"Hold him!" Pierre commanded as he slammed the door leading into the dungeons and bolted it shut. The area was immediately thrown into complete darkness. "Don't let him get away!"

Josef swore as he grappled with the man.

Pierre pulled a flashlight from his overcoat pocket and shone it in their captive's face. "We have you now," he growled in an evil voice, "it is no use struggling."

Mary Ellen was getting frantic. Most of the other tour members had already completed their shopping and reboarded the bus. She didn't know what was keeping Ty. She'd found a clock, she could see it through the gift shop window. She'd give him precisely three minutes to show up, and then she was calling in the guards.

The flashlight Pierre was holding wavered as the beam of light illuminated the man's face, revealing for the first time the fact that the man Josef was holding was not Tyler Stevenson.

"Josef, release him!"

"What?"

"You fool! Release him, I said. At once!"

Josef obeyed the command as he, too, noticed the official guard uniform that the man was wearing.

"I'm so sorry about this mix-up," Pierre apologized with overwhelming profuseness. He contritely smoothed the guard's disheveled clothing and bent down to retrieve the hat which had fallen to the ground during the struggle. "I can explain, I assure you. . . ."

Mary Ellen had had it with waiting. She was just about to head off for the dungeons herself when she realized she had no idea where they were. At that moment she caught sight of a group of guards. They could give her directions, even accompany her there. Yes, she liked that idea. She approached them. "Excuse me, could you help—"

One guard muttered something into his walkie-talkie and then all the guards rushed right past her without saying a word. Something had obviously happened. To Ty?

Mary Ellen closed her eyes in dismay. "I knew it, I knew something was wrong!"

"What makes you say that?" she heard Ty's voice say.

Her eyes flew open. "You're alive!" She didn't know whether to hug him or hit him.

"Of course I'm alive." He looked at her as if she'd taken leave of her senses. "Why shouldn't I be?"

"Because you visited the dungeons."

"I didn't know that was a capital offense," he said in a dry voice.

Mary Ellen was in no mood to appreciate his humor. "It ought to be. You scared me half to death; you were gone ages and then all these guards raced by. What happened?"

Ty shrugged his shoulders. "I was just about to enter the dungeons when someone slammed the door in my face. I waited around for a while to see if the guard who'd gone down ahead of me was going to reopen the place. Then I gave up and came back here. I guess the dungeons must have closed early today. Were you worried about me?"

Mary Ellen didn't answer his question; she didn't have to because the look in her eyes said it all.

"You *were* worried." His statement held a certain amount of satisfaction.

"It's a natural reaction," she retorted defensively. "You disappear and the guards race out of here like World War Three has just been declared. What do you think happened?"

"Beats me. Something must be rotten in the state of Denmark," he suggested.

"Whatever it was, we don't have time to find out right now," she said. "Come on, we've got to hurry or the bus will leave without us."

"Marielle . . ." He put his hand on her arm, halting her departure. "One thing first."

"What?" She turned her face up to his.

He kissed her, briefly but intensely. "Thanks for caring."

She did care. Too much.

"You'd better let me do the talking," Pierre muttered to Josef as they were both led away from the dungeon by a contingent of guards.

"But what about our . . . job?"

"We'll take care of him later. How hard can it be to follow a bus tour?"

108

CHAPTER SEVEN

"I'm going to die." Josef moaned as he leaned over the ship's railing.

Another wave buffeted the ferry making the crossing from Denmark to the northern coast of West Germany. A moment later Pierre joined Josef railside as his stomach also protested the tossing motion of the boat. They moaned in unison as their *mal de mer* got the better of them.

Inside the ferry's enclosed cabin the other passengers were faring much better than Pierre and Josef.

"I'm glad you gave me that antiseasickness pill," Sheldon told Irma. "I haven't been on a ship since World War Two, but I can still remember how sick I got."

"How about you?" Ty softly asked Mary Ellen.

"I'm fine." She'd never suffered from motion sickness.

"No, I meant do you remember the last time you were on a ship?"

"It was a sailboat, not a ship, and it was seven years ago on Lake Michigan," she reluctantly recalled.

"You were with me."

"That's right." Ty had promised her a sailing trip out on the lake in his father's boat, but they'd ended up spending the afternoon down in the cabin. Although the sailboat had never left its mooring, Mary Ellen had been swept away by a riptide of passion.

Memories of Ty's lovemaking were continually eroding her determination. Last night she'd lain awake, listening to the even cadence of Ty's breathing as he slept and remembering how good it had been between them seven years ago.

Her voice of logic tried to insist that her memories might well be tinged with the romantic illusions that often made the past seem better than it actually was. But her heart told her that the dangerous pleasure she felt at his lightest caress was no figment of idealized memories. He had only to touch her and she was melting inside. Quite simply Ty was hazardous to her self-control.

Outside on the ferry's upper deck Pierre and Josef were struggling to regain their self-control as they finally straightened from their bent position over the railing.

"I thought we were lucky to get away from Denmark without charges being filed for that little mix-up at the castle." Pierre gasped. "But now I'm not so sure."

Josef wearily agreed. "The dungeon . . . may have been dark . . . but at least . . . the floor . . . did not keep . . . moving . . . this way!"

Pierre groaned and rushed back to the railing. As far as he was concerned they couldn't reach the shores of Germany soon enough.

A new bus and driver met the tour group in Puttgarden, West Germany. Christian supervised the clearing of German customs and herded everyone on board the bus, counting heads before giving the okay for the driver to proceed to their night's lodging in Hamburg.

The day was cold and blustery, as if Mother Nature had decided to turn back the meteorological calendar from spring to winter. The weather matched her mood, Mary Ellen gloomily decided as she viewed the racetrack-like speeds of the passing cars on the German autobahn.

Her mood was not improved any by the envious looks that Ty was giving to the speeding Mercedes and Porsches as they whizzed by the much slower-moving bus.

"You're missing life in the fast lane, aren't you?" she demanded with a gesture toward the window, where yet another Porsche went roaring by. "That's where you belong, isn't it? Out there where there are no speed limits!"

"I'll admit this is a change of pace for me. And you're absolutely right." He paused to take her hand before continuing his confession. "I *was* wishing I were somewhere else." Ty lifted her hand to his lips and lowered his voice to a roughly seductive whisper. "I was wishing I were in bed, the same bed, with you." His tongue teased the inside of her wrist. "Wishing that I were making love to you, that I were kissing your bare skin, tasting you all over."

She snatched her hand away. "Stop that!"

His look was positively wicked. "What's wrong, Marielle? Getting worried that you're not going to be able to hold out?"

"That's ridiculous."

"Is it?"

"Yes."

He ran a finger down her neck to the base of her throat, where the open collar of her blouse allowed him access to the pulse beating there. "Still denying what we've got going between us?"

Mary Ellen drew in a large breath and held it a moment while willing her heartbeat back to normal. Satisfied that she would now be able to speak coherently, she said, "I'm simply requesting that you abide by the rules."

"Rules and I never got along well—you know that, Marielle." Ty couldn't resist dropping a fleeting kiss to her lips, thereby softening their disapproving line. "Under the circumstances I think I'm doing extremely well by restraining myself to such a degree."

"You call kissing me every two seconds being restrained?" she demanded in exasperation.

"It isn't every two seconds," he denied with a grin, "although I am tempted. I do agree with you in one respect, though. There's nothing at all restrained about the way you respond to my kisses."

"Stolen kisses are not going to change my mind," she loftily informed him.

"Changing your mind is a woman's prerogative," he reminded her.

"Not this woman's."

"Know what I think?"

"No, and I don't want to."

Ty proceeded nonetheless. "I think that you're afraid I'm getting too close." He laced his fingers through hers.

She shifted away from him. "You are too close. Please don't complicate things, Ty."

His thumb soothingly stroked the back of her hand. "I'm not trying to complicate things; you are. I want to simplify. One bed, instead of two."

"Simpler for you, maybe. Not for me."

Exasperated by her continued denials Ty began losing his patience. "You're still mad at me for leaving Chicago so abruptly, is that it?"

"That's part of it, yes."

"I've already explained about that."

"You've always got an explanation," she muttered under her breath.

113

Ty didn't hear her. "Marielle, you're making mountains out of molehills. Why let a small misunderstanding stand in the way of our happiness now?"

"Because I can't accept happiness now knowing I'll have to pay the price later on."

"Taking chances is part of being alive, but the rewards are well worth the risks. Think about it, Marielle."

She did think about it as the bus ate up the miles between Germany's northern coastline and the city of Hamburg. She was no closer to reaching a decision when they arrived at their hotel than she had been when they'd started out. All that thinking had only served to give her a headache.

Mary Ellen wasn't the only one feeling somewhat under the weather. Pierre and Josef, still recovering from their severe bout of seasickness, had been attempting to catch up with Ty and the rest of the bus tour all afternoon. Only now that it was almost dark did they finally pull into the hotel parking lot. By then the two men were so exhausted that they could barely get out of the tiny car they'd rented in Copenhagen.

"Ohhh! The ground is still moving!" Josef announced in dismay as he attempted to walk on rubbery legs.

"Nonsense. It is all in your mind," Pierre stated, although he, too, moved like a drunken sailor.

"My mind?" Josef repeated. "No, it is definitely my stomach that is aching."

"Come along and quit complaining. We must make sure that this hotel is indeed where Stevenson is staying."

"But you said when we lost them on the autobahn that you already knew where the bus was going."

"Enough of your chatter. Just follow me and stay out of sight."

Their slinking entry into the hotel lobby went unnoticed amid the hustle and general confusion as the tour group stood around waiting for their rooms to be assigned and their luggage to be brought in.

"Quick, there he is!" Pierre hissed as he spied Ty across the lobby. "Don't let him see you!"

Pierre grabbed Josef by the collar of his ill-fitting trench coat and hauled him behind the nearest available shelter, which turned out to be a luggage cart that was perilously overloaded. Josef knocked into the side of the cart, toppling over an avalanche of suitcases. Alarmed at the possibility of getting caught Pierre and Josef fled out a side door.

Mary Ellen was searching for her passport in her purse when she heard the sudden commotion on the other side of the lobby. The next thing she knew she was being hauled into Ty's arms. She was about to protest his sudden burst of ardor when she realized that he hadn't been motivated by passion or lust. This embrace was different. He was prepared for trouble, but then she felt the tension in him relax as Ty realized that there was no evident threat to their safety.

"What's going on?" Mary Ellen's demand was muffled by his shirtfront. He'd tugged her to him with such force that she was practically plastered against him.

Ty loosened his hold on her, allowing her to free her face. "It looks like there was an accident with the luggage." He checked the gathering crowd for the two men who had been clumsily tailing him back in Copenhagen, but saw no sign of them. Dismissing his suspicions as being unfounded Ty finally released Mary Ellen.

"I thought they'd piled that cart too high," Mitzi was stating with a knowing nod. "I was afraid something like this would happen."

"I hope they didn't break my cosmetic case," someone else could be heard to say.

"I hope no one's been hurt," Viola said with a glare in the direction of the person who'd worried about their cosmetic case.

Someone was hurt—Christian. Hank, who'd been standing next to the tour guide before the accident, knelt beside Christian and diagnosed a broken ankle. A doctor was duly dispatched and Hank's diagnosis was confirmed. Christian did indeed have a broken ankle and would not be able to continue as the group's guide.

"Poor Christian," Irma exclaimed.

"What do we do now?" Sheldon wondered.

"Go home?" Archie suggested with visions of tacos and chili dogs running through his head.

"Thank heavens I brought my own guidebook," Mitzi murmured, thereby earning a glare from Viola.

As he was being carried away on a stretcher, Christian was still heroically thinking of his responsibility to the tour group as he requested that no one panic. "There will be someone here in the morning to take over for me," he promised as he was being loaded into an ambulance.

"Ty, you don't think Christian's accident had anything to do with the people chasing you, do you?" Mary Ellen couldn't help asking in a troubled undertone.

Ty firmly allayed her worries. "I don't see how it could. We weren't standing anywhere near that luggage cart. No, it must have been just an unfortunate accident."

The hotel manager made sure there were no more mishaps for the tour group by quickly handing out their room keys himself.

The moment they were inside their room, Mary Ellen headed for the bed.

A naughty glitter lit Ty's brown eyes as he teased, "Marielle, I'm shocked! At least give me time to take off my jacket before we head for bed!"

Knowing how dangerously appealing he was when he used that tone of voice, she deliberately avoided looking at him and instead centered her attention on the bed's construction.

117

"Aha! This is a pair of twin beds just like the ones we had in Copenhagen."

"You sound relieved," he chided her. "You weren't worrying about tonight's sleeping arrangements by any chance, were you?"

"Worried?" she repeated with a mocking shake of her head. "About sleeping next to a wolf? Why should I be worried?"

"Maybe I'm just a sheep in wolf's clothing," he suggested with a look of bland innocence.

"And maybe pigs can fly," she retorted. "Now, are you going to move the furniture, or shall I?"

Ty gently shoved her out of the way. "I'll do it." He kissed her first, though. "To give me strength," he explained with a jaunty grin.

As Ty bent over to move the bed, she watched the play of his muscles beneath the thin cotton of his shirt. She was getting to be quite good at watching him without appearing to do so, but she wasn't sure it was an art at which she wanted to excel. She wasn't supposed to want to watch him. She wasn't supposed to want him, period. But she did. She was the one who needed strength!

Mary Ellen was quiet and withdrawn for the remainder of the evening. Remembering the lingering looks the handsome tour guide had given Mary Ellen, Ty attributed her silence to anxiety about Christian. Ty hadn't forgotten her announced intention of having a fling while in Europe, and he wondered if her si-

118

lence was a result of disappointment that Christian was now out of the picture.

Ty continued to study Mary Ellen as they ate dinner in the hotel's restaurant. What exactly was it about this one woman that fascinated him so? What was it about her that he hadn't been able to find in anyone else? He only knew that he wanted her so much he actually ached for her; not only physically, but in some other way that was totally foreign to him. A more communicative man might share his feelings. Ty simply clammed up.

It was unusual for Ty to be silent, and Mary Ellen noticed. Was he worried about his situation, about the men who were following him? Or, she wondered, was he plotting some new game plan in his seduction schemes?

Mary Ellen was still wondering as she prepared for bed later that evening. She was also wondering how she was going to wash her hair without a shower. She didn't have much choice —she'd have to wash her hair in the sink—so, under the circumstances, she decided to get the job over with tonight instead of in the morning.

In the other room Ty lay sprawled out on his bed, a deck of cards spread out before him. The sleight of hand he was absently performing ended up in a mess as he heard a crash from the bathroom, followed by the unusual sound of Mary Ellen swearing.

"What's going on in here?" he demanded as he opened the bathroom door, which Mary Ellen had forgotten to lock. "What are you doing with your head in the sink?"

"I'm trying to wash my hair," she snapped while blindly reaching out in search of the bottle of shampoo she'd placed on the shelf beside the sink. She'd already knocked over a tube of toothpaste and a stick of deodorant in her futile quest.

Without saying a word Ty poured a capful of shampoo into the palm of his hand and set to work, lathering her wet hair into a veritable pyramid of bubbles. The feel of his strong fingers moving over her scalp was disturbingly pleasurable. He worked from her nape upward to the crown of her head and down the sides to her temples.

"What are you doing?" she demanded when his massaging became more abstract.

"I'm sculpting." Ty swirled the frothy mass into the shape of a pair of horns, smoothed it back, and got another idea. "Want to see how you look with a beard?"

"No. If you're going to help me, you can rinse off the shampoo before I'm permanently bent into this shape."

Ty selfishly took a moment to study her shape as she leaned over the sink. The slacks she was wearing clung to the curve of her bottom in a most alluring manner. Her blouse was some sort of silky material that was already wet along the collar where he'd inadvertently dripped water onto it. "You'd better take off

120

your blouse," he decided as he wiped his soapy hands on a towel. "It's getting all wet."

"That's all right. It's drip-dry."

"Now, Marielle, don't be timid." Since her blouse fastened down the back, Ty took it upon himself to efficiently undo the buttons. "Careful," he advised when she jerked upright. "You'll get soap in your eyes and a blouse at your feet."

Realizing the truth of his words Mary Ellen hastily bent over again. "You don't have to unbutton the blouse all the way down to my waist!" she angrily informed him.

"I suppose you're right." He sighed regretfully and left the last few buttons secured. "You've got a lovely back, you know." He traced a finger up her spine and over her shoulder blade. "Creamy skin with a light scattering of freckles." He placed several kisses across her exposed flesh.

Mary Ellen shivered. Goose bumps rose along her arms. "Are you going to help me or not?" Her demand was made in a strangled voice.

"Why, Marielle, I thought I was helping you," he murmured into her ear.

"I'm cold."

He ran his hand along her shoulder. "Funny, you don't feel cold."

Mary Ellen was on the verge of turning on the water and submerging her head under the faucet when Ty stopped his sensual teasing and rinsed off the shampoo for her. In short order he wrapped a towel around her head and pulled her upright.

The movement caused her blouse to slip off her shoulders, which in turn caused Ty to swallow and grit his teeth as a wave of desire surged through his body. He abruptly shoved the hair dryer into her hands. "Here, you'd better do the rest yourself. I'm going to take a shower."

A moment later Mary Ellen found herself on the other side of the now closed and locked bathroom door, the sound of running water announcing the fact that Ty had turned on the bath water. A slight smile lifted her lips as she remembered that there was no shower, which was why she'd had to wash her hair in the sink in the first place!

Ty obviously hadn't been thinking clearly. Sexual tension could do that to a person. She should know. She felt that way whenever Ty was within shouting distance. It was only fair that he should get a taste of his own medicine.

Besides, he was the one who'd started things. Everything would have been fine if he hadn't barged into the bathroom and taken it upon himself to start undressing her. She stubbornly ignored the inner voice which reminded her that the sexual tension between them had started years ago and had never really stopped.

Determined to be in bed feigning sleep by the time Ty was out of the bathroom, Mary Ellen hurriedly blew her hair dry. Speed rather than styling was her main concern, and she did manage to get between the sheets before Ty rejoined her in their bedroom. Sleep, however, was not as easily achieved.

It began with Ty muttering when he came out of the bathroom and found the bedroom darker than the ace of spades. His muttering soon turned to swearing as he hit his knee on a low luggage rack that stood directly in his path.

She spoke hesitantly into the darkness. "Are you all right?"

His growled "No" was not exactly reassuring.

Mary Ellen reached out to turn on the bedside lamp. Shielding her eyes from the sudden glare of light, she sent a squinting look in Ty's direction. He was sitting on the corner of her bed. He'd rolled up one trouser leg of the dark-blue silk pajama bottoms and was inspecting the damage done to his knee.

Some latent Florence Nightingale trait came to the fore, prompting Mary Ellen to leave the safe confines beneath the covers and venture out to nurse the wounded hero. "Here, let me look at it."

Ty leaned back, propping himself on his bent elbows. "Be my guest."

Her intentions were good, but her thoughts were naughty. Ty was now provocatively sprawled out on her bed. The clean scent of his soap mingled with the smell of freshly laundered sheets. It was easy to imagine the two of them crawling under those sheets.

Cool it, she silently ordered herself as she briskly checked his knee for abrasions. Everything felt and looked wonderful to her. So wonderful that her fingers lingered to soothe the warmth of his skin while she admired the shape of his knee.

"Feel free to check out the rest of me," Ty softly invited her.

His words snapped Mary Ellen out of her dreamy reverie. "That won't be necessary," she retorted, jerking her fingers away from him and clenching them into fists. "Your injury isn't serious, I'm sure you'll live."

"Yes, but will I ever play the piano again?" He wiggled his eyebrows at her in the manner of a vaudeville comedian.

Even though the joke was an old one, Mary Ellen laughed.

"I've missed your laughter," Ty murmured.

Mary Ellen knew she was on dangerous ground and decided it was time for a tactical retreat. "Since you've made yourself so comfortable on my bed, you can stay there. I'll sleep on the other bed."

The arrangement proved unsatisfactory for both of them. Mary Ellen was kept awake by visions of Ty sprawled amid the sheets she'd already warmed, while Ty was haunted by the elusive scent of Mary Ellen's cologne that still clung to the pillow.

A new battle plan occurred to Ty the next morning when he, and the rest of the tour group, met their beautiful interim tour guide —a lively and shapely brunette named Gina. The plan came to him when he saw the inviting look Gina gave him over breakfast and noticed the resultant glare Mary Ellen gave Gina.

Jealousy was a good sign, surely? he thought to himself.

Ty didn't actually go out of his way to flirt with Gina, he simply allowed her to flirt with him. The difference was too fine lined for Mary Ellen to appreciate, however. The situation worsened when Gina made a special point of stopping next to Ty during lunch and placing her hand on his shoulder.

"If there's anything I can do for you, Mr. Stevenson, anything at all, you be sure and let me know," Gina murmured in a sexy voice.

"Call me Ty," he replied with a grin.

"Call him unreliable," Mary Ellen muttered to herself.

As they embarked on a city tour of Hamburg, Mary Ellen was immersed in her own thoughts and her own battles. She tried telling herself that she had no cause to feel jealous, that she had no hold on Ty. It didn't work. Each time Gina smiled at Ty, Mary Ellen felt a stab of angry resentment. Each time Gina touched Ty's arm or shoulder, Mary Ellen wanted to punch her.

Gina was a good guide, with a lively wit and a natural way of dealing with people. With the exception of Mary Ellen everyone liked her and was sorry to hear that, once the bus reached Frankfurt for the night, Gina would be leaving them to lead her own regularly scheduled tour group.

"Worldwind Tours has arranged for a permanent replacement to join your group," Gina told them. "She will be waiting for you when we arrive at the hotel outside Frankfurt."

Mary Ellen sourly wished for a tour guide who would be eligible for social security and ineligible for any kind of beauty contest. Her wish was granted. Their new tour guide, Bertha, was a stoutly built woman whose manner and appearance were both military in nature. It came as no surprise to hear Bertha barking commands instead of offering suggestions.

"She gives new meaning to the word *battle-ax*," Viola told Mary Ellen in a whisper.

Mary Ellen's reply was distracted, for she had more important things on her mind, mainly her increasing vulnerability where Ty was concerned. She kept hearing his assertion that he wouldn't make love to her until she asked him to. She also kept seeing the double bed in their room upstairs. Her luck had run out.

She wasn't about to give in without a fight, and having so decided, she hurried back to her room and dug out the card of the businessman she'd sat next to on the flight over from the States.

Philip Ramsey. She studied his handwriting. The phone number he'd written was easy to read, but difficult for her nervous fingers to dial.

She didn't have much time. Ty was still down

in the lobby, buying a newspaper, but he'd be back soon.

Philip Ramsey answered on the first ring.

"This is Mary Ellen Campbell—we shared the same flight from Chicago to London a week ago," she reminded him.

"Mary Ellen!" He sounded pleased. "I'm glad you called. I hope this means you're finally going to accept my dinner invitation?"

She took a deep breath and nervously launched into speech. "That's right. I am calling to accept your invitation, Philip."

"Wonderful. How has your trip been so far?"

"Wonderful," she parroted.

"Peachy keen," Ty sneered from the doorway.

"I'll pick you up at your hotel," Philip was saying, unaware that Mary Ellen was sitting frozen at the other end of the line. "Where are you staying?"

Philip's last question was voiced in midair as Ty grabbed the receiver out of Mary Ellen's hand.

"She's staying with me," Ty brusquely announced. "And she's going to be staying with me all night, so you can just forget about any invitations. The lady's not available."

Ty hung up before either Mary Ellen or Philip Ramsey could say another word.

"How dare you!" she sputtered, so angry she could hardly speak.

Ty's temper matched hers. "How dare I? How dare you! The minute my back is turned you start making secret assignations with some strange man."

"Philip is not strange, and I was not making assignations. I was accepting a dinner invitation. Your hanging up the phone is not going to change that. I'll simply place the call again."

"No, you won't. You won't be calling, you won't be accepting any invitations, and you won't be leaving this room tonight."

Mary Ellen was tempted to say, *Wanna bet?* but she remembered that Ty was an experienced gambler and thought better of it.

While she waffled over what to say, Ty went on to tell her what she would be doing tonight. "You're staying with me and you're sharing that bed with me."

Mary Ellen knew he meant for her to be sharing a lot more than just the bed, but she refused to be intimidated. "You're jealous!" She threw the accusation at him, certain he'd deny it.

He didn't. "That's right."

"You've got no right to be jealous. You've got no rights over me."

"You want me. That gives me certain rights. I won't have you bringing a third person into this. This is between you and me, Marielle."

She neatly sidestepped his first allegation about wanting him and focused her anger on the last part of his statement. "You won't have *me* bringing a third person into this? Ha! What about you and Gina? It sounds to me like you want to have your cake and eat it too."

128

"I don't want cake, I want you."

"And Gina, and God only knows how many other women."

Ty angrily gripped her arms. "Whatever happened to the eighteen-year-old girl who thought I could do no wrong?" he demanded.

"She grew up into the twenty-five-year-old woman who knows better!"

"You don't know anything at all. You just think you do."

Mary Ellen slipped out of his grasp. "So now you're accusing me of being stupid, is that it?"

"No, that's not it. Don't try to change the subject."

"Stop ordering me around!"

The angrier she got, the calmer he got. "Maybe I will when you stop pretending that there's nothing between us."

"I'm not pretending."

"Aren't you?" He took a step closer. "Think again, Marielle. Think about the way your heart races when we're in the same room together." He caught hold of her hand and placed it on his chest. "Feel my heart—it's doing the same thing." The gentle roughness of his voice was seducing her as surely as the look in his eyes. "Think about the way you feel when I touch you. Think about how good it was between us. It can be that way again, Marielle. It will be that way again."

"No." Her denial was now a mere whisper.

Triumph flared in his eyes as he drew her closer. "Yes, Marielle."

His certainty that he'd won spurred her into action. "No!" Her voice was panicky. "I will not be twisted around your little finger this way! You can't seduce me with words and old memories!"

In a flash Mary Ellen had pulled away from him and raced into the bathroom. She'd slammed the door and locked it before he could make a move to stop her.

"Mary Ellen, open this door!"

There was no reply.

"Mary Ellen, I told you to open this door. Now!"

Still no reply.

"Damn it, answer me! Open this door before I break it down."

Silence.

"Did you hear me?"

"Go away." She turned on the shower.

Ty's roar was clearly audible even over the sound of the rushing water. "I'm giving you until the count of three to open this door, and then I'm going to break it down!"

Mary Ellen finished stripping and stepped into the shower. She needed to think. She needed to be sure. The decision had to be hers.

"One."

She lathered herself with a bar of scented soap.

"Two."

She rinsed herself off.

"Three. That's it. I'm coming in."

She stepped out of the shower.

The door shook as Ty rammed his shoulder against it.

Mary Ellen stared in the mirror and screwed up her courage.

Ty angrily rubbed his sore shoulder. He was no expert at locked doors; most had been voluntarily opened for him.

When this door finally opened Mary Ellen stood there wearing nothing but a smile.

CHAPTER EIGHT

Mary Ellen was disappointed by Ty's reaction. Instead of gazing at her with passionate longing, he was staring at her with unmistakable wariness.

She stood and waited for him to make the first move.

Her complete turnaround confused the hell out of him. "What is this?"

"It's me." She should have been nervous, she should have felt awkward standing there completely naked while Ty was still fully dressed. But she didn't, because she knew what she wanted, and she'd come to terms with her needs. Ty was right. She had been pretending. She had been fighting the magic. But no more. The battle was over.

Ty was still struggling to come to grips with this unexpected turn of events. When she'd locked herself in the bathroom he thought she'd gone off to sulk. Now he didn't know what to think. In fact he could barely think at all with her standing a mere foot away, looking even better than he could have imagined! And he had a vivid imagination where Mary Ellen was concerned.

During the nights he'd spent trying to sleep he'd wondered if she'd changed from the eighteen-year-old virgin he remembered. She most certainly had. The promise of beauty she'd possessed as a teenager was fulfilled in the woman she'd become.

Ty clenched his hands into fists to prevent himself from reaching for her, because he knew if he touched her he wouldn't be able to let her go, no matter how many times she told him to stop. "What kind of game are you playing now?"

"The kind of game where I get to seduce you for a change."

That did it. He gave up trying to make sense out of her behavior and gave in to his overwhelming need to touch her, to make sure she was for real. He reached for her with a groan. "You're crazy, do you know that?"

She shook her head, the wavy ends of her hair brushing across her bare shoulders. "Do you still want me?"

"You know I do." His deep voice swept over her like black velvet.

"Then why are you still wearing all these clothes?"

Ty swooped down to capture her sexy laughter with his mouth. He held her to him with one hand while feverishly working to undo his shirt buttons with the other. With Mary Ellen's help the shirt was soon off, and Ty sent it flying across the room.

Now there was nothing between her breasts and the muscled planes of his chest. She celebrated that fact by rubbing against him with the sensuousness of a sleek cat. Leaning against him she stretched and stood on tiptoes.

"Slow down!" He gasped. "You're burning me up! We've got all night." He placed a string of kisses across her face. "I don't want to rush this, I want to enjoy every inch of you. But first you've got to tell me." He tilted her chin until she was staring directly into his dark eyes. "What made you change your mind?"

She sighed and leaned her forehead on his shoulder. "I couldn't fight it any longer. But *I* had to be the one to decide that. I knew you were about to take me in your arms and convince me to change my no into a yes. I panicked. I knew you could make me change my mind, but I didn't know if I could live with that afterward. So I had to take a quick time out. *I* had to make the choice. Do you understand what I'm saying?"

"Not entirely, but I'm not exactly thinking clearly."

"Me either." She kissed his chin and nibbled on his neck. "It must be contagious."

"Must be," he agreed. "I know a cure." He swept her up in his arms and carried her to the double bed.

Mary Ellen lay where he'd set her and watched him finish undressing. Only now did she realize how long she'd waited for this moment. Her breath caught in her throat as he shucked his pants. Even though he was still wearing a pair of dark briefs, the state of his arousal was clearly evident.

Unable to read the fleeting emotions in her eyes, Ty opted to leave his briefs on as he joined her on the bed. "Don't get cold feet." His tone was both a command and a supplication.

"I'm not." She was shaking all over. "I just forgot how strong you are."

"Feel free to refresh your memory," he huskily invited her.

Mary Ellen hesitatingly reached out, her fingers resting on the already familiar expanse of his chest before slowly investigating the muscular ridges leading down to his navel. She loved the feel of him. Her lips explored the shadow of his five o'clock stubble while her hands stroked his hard abdomen. So smooth in one place, so rough in another.

Although her hands skimmed close to that part of him that throbbed with life, she skittishly avoided full contact. As it was he responded so intensely to her touch that she was concerned she might be causing him pain rather than pleasure. "Am I doing something wrong?" she whispered as he moaned.

"No. It's just that if you don't touch me I think I'll go crazy."

"But I am touching you."

"Touch me here." He gripped her hand and guided it to him.

She watched the passion flare in his dark eyes as she rested her palm on him. She was awed by the evidence of such power. Inspired by his response she became more adventurous, until her bewitching fingers nearly drove him frantic.

"Oh, Marielle!" Ty shuddered and rolled on top of her, pinning her beneath him. His mouth captured hers for a kiss that was raw with hunger. Her response was wild and free. When his tongue entered the sweet interior of her mouth, hers was there to greet it. His kissing created a wild intoxication that worked its way into every corner of her mind, shutting down coherent thought.

But that was nothing compared to what his hands were doing to her body. His prowling fingers were everywhere at once; their touch barely realized one place before moving on to another. A restless need for more burned within her, a fire fueled by his masterful touch. She shivered and arched into his embrace.

His tongue swirled around her ear as his hands cupped the sleek lushness of her breasts. He handled her with exquisite skill; he knew

136

exactly when and where to rub, skim, stroke, massage. When she was moaning with pleasure he shifted his hands around to her lower back, leaving her breasts open to the loving assault of his devilish tongue and seductive teeth.

Mary Ellen was inundated by primitive needs. Her face was flushed, her eyes brilliant with desire. Yet this was only the beginning.

Mary Ellen threaded her fingers through Ty's dark hair and held on as the tremors rocking her body were increased by the tugging motion of his mouth. Simultaneously his hands slid from her back to her hips before zeroing in on the one part of her that was silently aching to be touched. She gasped as his fingers began their intimate introduction. He ministered to her needs until she was overcome by the wild excitement he'd released within her.

Ty lifted his head and watched the pleasure he'd given her darken her eyes and light up her face. The feel of her convulsive movements threatened the last remnants of his own control. He freed her to peel his briefs away.

Mary Ellen blinked away the beads of sweat from her eyes and beheld the masculine beauty of him. He was incredible. Lean and muscular. Virile and fully aroused. Would she be able to please him?

"Don't worry," he murmured, mistaking her anxiety for concern about the need for precautions. "I'll take care of everything."

He did, and when he came back to her she welcomed him with open arms.

"You're so beautiful." He ran his hands along her body, from her trembling knees up to her shoulders and back again.

"So are you." She trailed her hands down his spine. She felt him tremble as her fingernails delicately scraped his bare skin.

Her actions loosened the reins on his restraint. "Oh, God. Hold on, honey. I . . . can't . . . wait any longer." With a surge of motion he came to her, swiftly positioning himself and thrusting.

It was almost as if it were the first time again. Afraid of hurting her Ty froze and prepared to withdraw. Sensing his imminent retreat Mary Ellen moaned. "No, don't leave me. Love me. Love me now."

The feel of her hands combined with the restless urging of her body served to dissolve Ty's qualms. With exquisite precision he completed their union, shuddering as she eagerly accepted all of him. He could feel the rippling tremors his gliding thrusts were creating within her.

Words were replaced by moans as an ever-tightening coil of anticipation took hold of her. Her expressive eyes, her breathing, her heart-beat, were all wild. His erotic combination of advance and retreat sent her spiraling upward. She was poised on the brink and Ty prolonged her pleasure until she thought she'd scream.

She gripped him with frantic hands as the tension abruptly exploded into undulating waves. Ty stiffened and tumbled over the edge

138

right along with her, both of them calling out words of love.

They lay in each other's arms, too sated to move. Eventually Ty kissed the very tip of her nose and shifted away from her. "I'm too heavy for you," he said when Mary Ellen murmured a sleepy protest.

She curled against him and was asleep in an instant.

Ty lay staring at the ceiling, unable to sleep because of the thoughts running through his head. Was it possible that Mary Ellen had not made love to another man since their summerlong affair? Had he been her only lover?

The possibility stunned him. On the one hand he was pleased at the idea of being Mary Ellen's only lover. On the other, he was confused by the discovery. She was a lovely woman. She was a passionate woman. Why would she deny herself for seven years? And why had she given in to him now?

Mary Ellen turned in her sleep and bumped into something warm and unyielding. Her eyes flew open before memory returned. Ty. She smiled.

Bracing herself on one elbow she squinted in the darkness to see if Ty was still sleeping.

"It's all right, I'm awake," he said.

"I'm sorry. Did I wake you?"

"No. I wasn't asleep."

"Why not? Is something wrong?"

Ty turned on the bedside light. "We need to talk."

Mary Ellen blinked against the sudden glare. Her trembling fingers shoved her angled bangs out of her eyes as she told herself not to panic. "What do you want to talk about?" she asked in a neutral tone.

He got right to the point. "Look, this may sound as egotistical as hell, but I could swear that you haven't been with a man for a long time."

"Why does it matter? Was I unsatisfactory?"

"Marielle, you were incredible, you know that."

"No, I don't know that. I wake up and find you waiting to cross-examine me. What am I supposed to think?"

"Come here." He pulled her to him. "You were fantastic." He went on in intimately sexy detail until Mary Ellen was blushing all over.

Determined to make Ty forget his curiosity about her previous experiences, or lack thereof, she whispered a sultry suggestion. "If I was that good, maybe we should do it again."

Ty didn't need any convincing. "I second the motion."

"This motion?" She brushed against him.

"That's the one."

They made love, dozed off, and made love again until the early hours of the morning.

When their wake-up call came at six A.M., Ty rolled over, lifted the receiver off the hook, stuffed it inside the bedside stand, and closed the door on it. A few minutes later Mary Ellen's alarm clock/calculator beeped in her purse,

140

where she'd left it the previous night. Neither she nor Ty even heard it. But they did hear a thunderous pounding on their door at seven A.M.

Ty shot bolt upright. "What the—"

"This is Bertha!" the tour guide bellowed. "You're holding up the rest of the tour. Report down to breakfast in ten minutes, the bus leaves at eight. If you're not on it, we'll leave without you."

"Go ahead," Ty retorted, but Bertha had already marched off.

Cringing with embarrassment Mary Ellen pulled the covers over her head.

A moment later Ty joined her. "Why are you hiding under here?"

"Why didn't you wake me up?"

"I did. Several times. During the night. Don't you remember?"

She refused to blush. "I meant this morning. How could you let us oversleep like this?"

"Me? What about you? Why didn't you wake me up?"

The absurdity of holding such a conversation under the covers got the better of her. She grinned and repeated his staccato delivery. "I did. Several times. During the night. Don't you remember?"

"I remember, all right. Every intimate detail, every erotic second, every satiny inch."

"Me too."

Ty leaned closer to trace the outline of her lips with the tip of his tongue. Mary Ellen's *mmmm* of pleasure blended right into their kiss. At first it was a mere brushing of mouths, back and forth, again and again. Then tantalizing nibbles were added. Before long passion flared yet again.

"Let's forget the tour bus," Ty huskily suggested.

Mary Ellen sighed and reluctantly moved away. "We can't." She had to struggle against the lingering temptation to stay in his arms. "Have you forgotten that you're on this tour for your own protection?"

Ty had forgotten.

Mary Ellen didn't wait for him to reply. "Come on, we've got to hurry. I'm going to go take a shower and wash my hair."

"I'll join you." He bounced out of bed after her. "It'll save time if we share."

"We'd only have time to share a shower and nothing else," she warned him. "We're late already."

Ty nodded. "Scout's honor," he agreed, but the gleam in his brown eyes said something else.

"You never were a boy scout."

"Get in the shower and stop arguing. Here, give me the soap." Ty ran the slippery bar all over her, working with tender efficiency. Mary Ellen reciprocated.

Despite their good intentions things in the shower were getting pretty steamy when their increasing passion was abruptly chilled by a torrent of frigid water.

Ty's curse mingled with Mary Ellen's shriek. He quickly released her to turn off the water.

"Tonight," Ty promised as he got out of the tub and dried himself with a bath towel. "I'm going to make love to you under the shower. *Before* the hot water runs out."

Mary Ellen gratefully accepted the towel he handed her. "What if our room doesn't have a shower?"

"I'll improvise."

"Mmmm, and you do it so well."

Bertha bammed on their bedroom door again. "Last call!"

Mary Ellen hastily dried her hair while Ty shaved and got dressed. She was easily side-tracked by the sight of him; his hair still damp from the shower, his face half-lathered with shaving cream, his body only partially clothed.

They arrived downstairs mere minutes before their final deadline. They didn't have time for breakfast, so they just grabbed coffee and Danish for the bus. There was barely time to load their luggage into the hold of the bus before they were hustled on board. Mary Ellen would have felt guilty at holding everyone up, but a glance at her watch told her that the bus was leaving right on time. That didn't matter to Bertha. Mary Ellen and Ty had interfered with her routine. She punished them with a glare.

Actually, now that Mary Ellen thought about it, she realized that Bertha never looked directly at you, she looked past you, usually over your right shoulder or at a point in the middle of your forehead. Strange. Mary Ellen later downgraded Bertha from being merely strange to being an absolute tyrant when two measly picture-taking stops were all the dictatorial tour guide allowed along the extremely photogenic Burgenstrasse, Germany's romantic Castle Road.

"Hurry," Bertha was forever ordering them. "We're behind schedule!"

"Whose schedule?" Sheldon demanded in a disgruntled undertone. "Not mine."

By the time they reached the city of Boppard, their departure city for the Rhine cruise, everyone was ready to collapse after having been rushed through lunch and then a city tour of Koblenz.

Pierre and Josef, still hot on Ty's trail, were also exhausted. And panic-stricken at the prospect of having to set foot on another boat.

"You have to do something!" Josef exclaimed in a frantic voice. "I cannot go on that boat. My stomach is still reeling from the last one."

"This is a river, not the sea," Pierre pointed out.

"I don't care. A boat is a boat."

"You're right." The bobbing motion of the docked boat was already making Pierre queasy.

"What are we going to do?"

"Give me a moment to think."

"Hurry, their guide is buying the tickets.

Maybe we should just grab Stevenson and make a run for it."

"No! I told you what our instructions were. Stevenson is not to know he is being followed. Our employer was quite emphatic on that point." Pierre recalled Mr. Q's interest at hearing that Stevenson had visited Elsinore, since Denmark's only casino was located near there. "Our employer thinks that Stevenson may be making contacts in an attempt to set up an operation of his own. We cannot afford to alert Stevenson now."

With such a restriction on time and options the best Pierre could come up with was detaining some member of the tour group. If one person from the group was missing, no one would be able to board. Tour groups worked like that, didn't they? All for one and one for all. Detain one and you detain them all.

Pierre quickly scanned his surroundings for some inspirations. He and Josef were standing near the washrooms. As he watched, one of the women from the tour bus headed their way.

Pierre grabbed hold of Josef's arm. "Quick, I have an idea. Listen. . . ."

Meanwhile Bertha was barking out a series of detailed instructions to her troop of weary tourists that ended with her ordering them all onto the steamer.

"I wonder what the penalties are for mutiny?" Sheldon muttered.

Bertha had herded most of the group onto the steamer before discovering that she was

145

short one member. She counted twice to be sure.

Irma, noticing Bertha's strange behavior, stopped on the gangplank before boarding the steamer. "What's wrong?"

"We are missing someone. No matter, we will find him later." Bertha waved away the problem and gestured for Irma and those few people behind her to move ahead. "Come along, get on board. The steamer is about to leave."

Hank surprised everyone by being the first to speak up. "Viola is missing. I'm not leaving without her."

"Neither are we," Sheldon stated on behalf of Irma and himself.

"The six of us will stay behind and look for Viola," Ty volunteered. "You go on ahead. We'll catch the next boat and meet you at the dock in Oberwesel."

"The group is not supposed to break up," Bertha argued.

"The group has already broken up," Ty retorted. "We're going to put it back together again. Don't worry about a thing. Just wait for us in the next port."

"All right, but you had better not be long or our schedule will be ruined."

Ty organized the makeshift search party into groups of two: Archie and Hank, Irma and Sheldon, himself and Mary Ellen. He assigned each pair an area of the dock to cover.

"Now what do we do?" Josef demanded as he watched the group spread out.

"Hide," Pierre replied.

Irma and Sheldon were quite pleased that they were the ones who located Viola. "Everyone, we found her!"

"Where is she?" Hank demanded in a worried voice. "Is she okay?"

"I'm locked in here," Viola could be heard to say through the thick door of the ladies' room.

Mary Ellen and Irma moved forward to go inside, but they were stopped by Ty, who barred their entrance with his arm. "Is anyone else in there with you, Viola?"

"Just me. The door to the stall is jammed. I can't get out."

Ty let his arm fall back to his side. "Don't worry, we'll have you out of there in a jiffy. I'll go get an official."

"Is that necessary?" Viola asked. "I'm already thoroughly embarrassed."

"Let Irma and me go in and see if we can't open the door," Mary Ellen suggested.

In the end it took two officials and a box full of tools to free Viola from her imprisonment. The officials apologized profusely.

"I don't think I've ever been so embarrassed in my life," Viola muttered. "How soon can we get out of here?"

"If we hurry we might be able to just make the next steamer," Ty said. "I don't trust Bertha to wait for us if we're too late."

147

They did just make the next boat. Pierre and Josef did not.

Pierre slapped his forehead and then hit Josef's arm. "Idiot!"

"What did I do?"

"You said she would be locked in there all day. Never mind, I have just gotten a brilliant idea." Pierre's frown was transformed into a smile. "I don't know why I didn't think of it earlier."

"Think of what?"

"We will drive to Oberwesel and meet the boat there. Hurry, to the car! We don't want to miss them!"

On board the steamer Ty, Mary Ellen, Irma, Sheldon, Hank, and Viola were all enjoying the scenery. Archie was enjoying his Sony Walkman.

"Look at all these castles. Aren't they something?" Sheldon murmured.

"I feel lost without Mitzi here to fill us in on what we're seeing," Irma had to admit.

As if in answer to her claim a voice came over the steamer's public announcement system and began reciting items of interest in both German and English. "The Rhine is truly a European river, for it travels through or borders on six different countries—Switzerland, Liechtenstein, Austria, Germany, France, and the Netherlands."

Even though the sun was shining, it was chilly out on the river. Shivering slightly Mary Ellen wrapped her arms around her middle.

The red Shaker knit sweater she wore over a white Oxford shirt wasn't windproof.

Seeing her discomfort Ty took off his leather jacket and slipped it over her shoulders. "Here, put this on. You'll be warmer."

She obediently slid her arms into the jacket's sleeves. The lining was still warm from his body. "What about you?" She looked at his thin pullover sweater in distress.

"The jacket will keep you warm, and you can keep me warm." His arms sneaked around her waist, and he tugged her to him until her back was resting against his chest.

Meanwhile a disembodied voice floated over the loudspeakers. "The most popular legend of the Rhine is that of the Lorelei, a maiden who lived on a steep and craggy rock and lured travelers to their deaths with her siren songs."

"I know a maiden who does the same thing in a shower," Ty whispered in Mary Ellen's ear.

The medieval town of Oberwesel, surrounded by walled towers dating back to the thirteenth and fourteenth centuries, was indeed one of the most picturesque places along the Rhine. Bertha stood on the dock, disapprovingly waiting for them. She didn't say a word, just gave them all her indirect glare and jerked her thumb toward the idling bus.

"What a welcome," Sheldon muttered with a very direct glare at Bertha.

Once they got on the bus, the lack of sleep the night before finally caught up with Ty and Mary Ellen. They both fell asleep in their seats as the bus headed for Heidelberg, their final destination for the night. It was dark when they were awakened by the sound of raised voices.

"What's going on?" Mary Ellen groggily asked.

Irma leaned across the aisle to supply the answer. "Bertha and the bus driver are arguing over the directions to our hotel. We should have reached it an hour ago, but Bertha has gotten us lost."

"Yeah," Sheldon leaned across Irma to join in the conversation. "Too bad you guys missed all the excitement."

"What excitement?" Ty questioned.

"The street Bertha told the driver to take was so narrow that the bus couldn't fit through it. Our poor driver had to back up. But the car behind us had some kind of engine trouble, and it stalled. So a bunch of guys, students from the university here, I think, just picked up the small car as if it were a toy. The funny thing was that the driver and passenger were still inside. Anyway, the guys set the car on the sidewalk and we backed up past it."

"We missed it by about a quarter of an inch," Irma inserted with a shudder.

"Yeah, I would have hated to be in that car," Sheldon agreed. "The poor driver and his passenger really looked shaken."

A few blocks away a still-shaken Pierre and Josef stood inside a yellow phone booth. "Who are you calling?" Josef asked Pierre.

"First I'm going to call the car rental agency and get us another car, a *big* one this time! And then I'm going to do what I should have done in the beginning. I'm going to call Worldwind Tours and get a copy of this damn tour's itinerary. There has got to be an easier way of following these people!"

CHAPTER NINE

That night Mary Ellen had nightmares about Bertha. They not only woke her, they also woke Ty, who was startled by her muffled groan.

"What's wrong?" He sounded sleepy and concerned.

"I'm sorry. I must have been dreaming." Mary Ellen sat up in bed. "It just seemed so real." She gave her pillow a few punches before stuffing it behind her and settling back against it. "And it was so strange. There was a mutiny on the bus. Our group turned into a mob and they tossed Bertha into the Rhine. Then they tossed the bus driver into the Rhine. And then you took over as the driver and we all started singing 'Ninety-nine Bottles of Beer on the Wall'!"

"Hmmm, that is strange." Ty laughed as he leaned up on one elbow. "But I think I know what it means."

"So do I. That I'm fed up with Bertha."

"Nope." Ty moved his leg over hers. He no longer bothered wearing pajamas to bed, preferring the silky feel of Mary Ellen's skin against his without any interference. "It sounds to me like your dream reflects a deep-seated need you have for me to make love to you."

"Where did you get an idea like that?"

"Right about here." Ty laid his palm over her heart.

She slid down next to him. "Mmmm, sounds good to me."

It felt good to her too!

After they made love Mary Ellen stayed close to Ty, her head resting on his shoulder as he slept. She had no illusions that this closeness would last. There was only one more week left of her dream vacation. When it was over Ty would be returning to his fast-paced life of racing and she would be returning to Chicago. She knew that.

Only one week. Mary Ellen resolved not to waste any of it in dreading the future. For the time being she'd adopt Ty's philosophy toward life—living and loving just for the moment. If only the moments wouldn't go by so quickly.

The next morning the tour proceeded south

from Heidelberg along yet another speedy autobahn. They arrived in Munich in time for an early lunch, and the sunny weather prompted the tour group to request that their lunch be served outside in the restaurant's authentic *biergarten*. But first they had to overcome Bertha's objections.

"We are supposed to eat inside."

Ty spoke for everyone when he asked why.

Bertha was not accustomed to having her decisions questioned. "Because that is the way it is scheduled."

"No, it isn't," Mitzi boldly contradicted her as she held up a copy of their tour brochure. "According to our agenda 'lunch, consisting of such Munich specialties as white sausages and pretzels, will be served outside in the *biergarten* if weather is permitting.' And I'd say the weather was permitting."

"So would I," Sheldon concurred.

Irma added her two cents' worth. "Look, they're even setting up a brass band."

"I'm not sure if an accordion player, a tuba player, and two trumpet players constitute a brass band," Ty murmured before wincing as Mary Ellen jabbed him with her elbow.

"Whose side are you on?" she demanded in a whisper.

"Yours," he whispered in return, making sure his fingers trailed around from her back to the side of her waist.

Mary Ellen grabbed hold of his hand before it reached more intimate territory.

Bertha eventually gave in to the group's request, but not before fixing them with one of her famous indirect glares and complaining, "It will take longer and we will be late for our tour of Munich."

They were indeed late, but not because of their eating outside in the *biergarten*. They were late because Bertha lost her sacred sheets of schedules. "No one is leaving until they are found!" Bertha announced over the lively sound of the Bavarian music. Her face took on a suspicious expression. "If this is someone's idea of a joke, I am not amused. If someone has taken the schedule sheets, they had better return them before any more time is lost."

Everyone in the group denied any knowledge of the whereabouts of her sacred schedule.

On the other side of the fence bordering the *biergarten*, Pierre was rapidly scribbling down the information listed on Bertha's sheets.

Josef took a moment's break as lookout to whisper, "Write faster! That guide has discovered that the sheets are missing. She is making everyone look for them."

"I'm hurrying, I'm hurrying," Pierre muttered. "There." He shoved the two sheets of paper over to Josef.

"What am I supposed to do with this?"

"Return it."

"Why me?"

"Because you are taller than I. You can see when no one is looking and then you can reach over the fence and let the papers drop. The guide will think the wind blew the papers off her table. She will never suspect a thing."

For once Pierre was absolutely correct. Neither Bertha nor anyone else suspected any foul play once Archie found the papers—on the ground near the tuba player's feet.

Bertha accepted her crumpled schedule sheets with a frown and no word of thanks. Seeing everyone milling around she bustled into action. "Well, what are you all standing around for? Hurry onto the bus, we are late."

They hurried but they still missed the display of the Glockenspiel in Munich's Marienplatz.

Mitzi was particularly heartbroken at the discovery. "But our tour description says we'll get to see the Glockenspiel!" She looked ready to cry.

Bertha was indifferent to Mitzi's disappointment. "You can see it. It is right there." She pointed to the tower of the town hall.

"But what about the display? Two levels of performing figures are supposed to come out, knights on horseback and folk dancers, and they revolve to the music."

Bertha shrugged. "If we had eaten inside we would not have had this problem. Anyway, it's just an oversized music box," Bertha continued defensively. "Besides we'll be stopping at a cuckoo clock factory later in the tour."

Mitzi was unappeased. "What's that got to do with anything?"

"There you will get to see plenty of things that revolve to the music at the stroke of the hour."

"Sounds like another substitution to me," Irma noted.

Sheldon agreed. "Yeah, like switching the 'Heidelberg By Night' tour for the 'Visit to a Zurich Casino.'"

Bertha repeated her explanation. "By the time we found our hotel last night it was too late to go on the 'Heidelberg by Night' tour."

Mary Ellen had to secretly confess to looking forward to visiting a real casino. She'd never been to one before—unlike Ty, who probably spent half his spare time there, when he wasn't racing. Jennifer had told her that because of their father's critical heart condition Ty had pulled out of several upcoming races this year, which no doubt gave him even more time to spend in the casinos.

The sound of Bertha's piercing voice cut into Mary Ellen's thoughts. "Follow me. Keep moving. . . ."

"This tour is beginning to resemble a marathon race, not a vacation," Mary Ellen heard Sheldon grouse as she caught up to the group.

The marathon continued as the tour left Munich for Innsbruck. The bus driver got into another argument with Bertha, this time over which route to take. They were speaking in French, which Ty was able to translate. To no one's surprise Bertha won the argument and they took the autobahn to Innsbruck instead of traveling on a more scenic route.

There was a short delay at the border between Germany and Austria while the officials perused the passports Bertha had collected and handed over. Upon reaching Innsbruck, Bertha directed the driver to let them all off in the center of town to save time. He was then to proceed to their hotel, a few blocks away, and supervise the unloading of the group's luggage.

Bertha kept up a frenetic pace that turned a walking tour of Innsbruck into a running relay match, with the person ahead trying to notify the person behind which way the rest of the tour group had gone.

The scenery was too breathtaking for Mary Ellen not to pause and share it with Ty.

She was not the only one who rebelled against Bertha's hurry-scurry march. Irma and Sheldon, Hank and Viola, even Mitzi and Archie, all stopped to admire the view down Maria-Theresienstrasse.

"Isn't this something?" Sheldon said.

Mary Ellen agreed. "It's beautiful. Look how the mountains rise straight up from the city. I had no idea they were so high!"

"According to my guidebook this is one of the most photographed scenes in Europe," Mitzi commented. "Uh-oh. Where's Bertha gone?"

Ty spoke for them all when he said, "I don't know, and I don't care."

"Mitzi, with your guidebook you could give

us as good a tour of Innsbruck as Bertha could," Irma suggested. "And you wouldn't walk us as fast."

"She did have us walking so fast that we couldn't even look around," Mitzi murmured, as if to convince herself to agree.

"What do you say?" Sheldon asked her.

"Okay, it's a deal. We'll probably get into trouble with Bertha for wandering off, though," Mitzi warned them.

Sheldon shrugged. "Who cares?"

No one did.

Irma's suggestion turned out to be an excellent one. Mitzi was in fact a better guide than Bertha. What she lacked in experience she made up for with enthusiasm.

Kind of like me, Mary Ellen thought to herself with a grin.

Aside from the scenery Mary Ellen's favorite part of the brief walking tour was the Little Golden Roof, which, according to legend and Mitzi's guidebook, had originally been covered with pure gold by Friedrich the Penniless to disprove the belief that he was poor.

Since the tourist sight was the last stop on Mitzi's unofficial tour, Ty took Mary Ellen by the hand and briskly led her away from the others.

"Where are we going?" she asked him.

"I've got a surprise for you, and I think we've got just about enough time—" Ty broke off his explanation as a taxi he'd hailed pulled over to the curb. Bundling Mary Ellen inside he gave the driver instructions and got them to their destination in short order.

When Ty hurried her out of the taxi, Mary Ellen complained. "You're beginning to act like Bertha, always rushing."

"So long as I don't look like Bertha," he retorted with a grin and a speedy kiss.

"I don't think you have to worry about that," she murmured.

"Good. And you don't have to worry about this." He stepped away from her and swept his hand toward the cogwheel-railway terminus. "You'll love it. Come on, one's just leaving." Ty hurriedly bought their tickets and hustled her on board before she had time to think. "Here, sit down by the window. And get your camera ready. The view is really great, especially when it's clear like this."

The cogwheel railway was crowded even at that relatively late hour of the afternoon. "A lot of people like to hike down," Ty told Mary Ellen when she commented on the number of people on board. "There are quite a few hours of daylight left yet."

"We're not hiking down, I hope?" She was alarmed at the prospect.

"No, not this time."

She sighed in relief. "Good, because my feet are already sore from all the hiking Bertha has had us doing the past few days."

"I've gone skiing all day and not been as tired as I have been from sightseeing," Ty confessed. "This tourist stuff is hard work!"

"Bertha makes it even harder."

"She certainly does." Ty leaned closer and blew in her ear. "She makes it hard for me to fool around with you."

Mary Ellen lifted her head in a gesture of teasing disapproval. "Fool around?"

"Yeah, you know. A little of this"—he kissed her neck—"a little of that"—he traced the curve of her ear with his finger.

Despite the fact that she and Ty had become lovers, his simplest touch still had the power to move her deeply. Her passion for him had not been appeased, her love for him had not diminished. But she was no longer a romantic eighteen-year-old and she knew that love and passion weren't always enough. Especially when that love was one sided. For although Ty had said he wanted her, and even said he needed her, he hadn't said he loved her.

In a way she was grateful for that. It was worse when he'd said he loved her that fateful summer and left her anyway. He couldn't give her what he didn't have, and that was the ability to make a commitment. This time she wasn't going to fool herself into believing otherwise.

"Hey, come back to earth," Ty murmured. "This is where we get off."

"Are we at the top?"

"No, this is"—he paused to read the sign—"the Hungerburg station."

While Mary Ellen was busy taking a series of panoramic photographs, Ty was busy checking out the departure time of the next cable car going even higher.

"Higher?" Mary Ellen repeated when he told her the news. "But there's snow up there."

"So? We're not going to be staying, we're just going to admire the view and come back down again."

"I don't know." She looked up at the snowy peaks and down at the clothes she was wearing. "I'm really not dressed for it."

"Just put your sweater on and you'll be fine." He was simultaneously guiding her arms into her bulky angora cardigan and urging her forward. "We won't be up there that long. But if we don't get a move on, we won't get up there at all."

"Why's that?"

"Because this is just about the last cable car going up. Come on, step in."

Mary Ellen did, but she wasn't wild about the way the cable car swung beneath her feet. And this was while it was still in dock, so to speak. She could only imagine what it would be like once they were hanging suspended from a mere cable of steel.

Suddenly this didn't seem like such a great idea, but it was too late to change her mind. The car operator had joined them and had already slid the door shut and fastened it securely. The operator pushed a button on the panel near the door, nodded at the man in what looked like a glass-encased control booth, and they were off.

"What do you think? Isn't this great?" Ty was in his element.

"Wonderful."

"Marielle, you have to open your eyes to really appreciate the view."

"I will, I will. Just give me a second." Actually reality turned out to be less terrifying than her imagination had prefigured it to be. As the cable car quietly carried them up above the tree line to the snowfields of the upper peaks, Mary Ellen looked down at the scenic vista spread out before her. She was enthralled by the miniature appearance of Innsbruck in comparison to the soaring, pine-covered slopes and precipitous mountains.

"Awesome, isn't it? Byron called these peaks 'the palaces of nature.'"

Mary Ellen looked at Ty in surprise. "I didn't know you read Byron. I didn't even know you liked poetry."

"I don't as a rule. The credit has to go to Mitzi and her guidebook. She read that quote to me and I liked it."

"So do I. I can't get over the contrasts between Innsbruck and the green valley down there and all of this snow up here."

The brilliant glare of the sun against the snow made Mary Ellen glad she'd brought along her sunglasses. Ty also slipped on a pair of dark aviator glasses which complimented his battered leather jacket. To her eyes he looked even better than the breathtaking scenery, and that took some doing!

"I'm glad you brought me up here," Mary Ellen said when they'd reached the end of the ride.

"We're not at the top yet. There's another cable car that goes up from here."

"Another one?"

The same operator who had taken them up on the previous cable car operated the second one. Again Ty and Mary Ellen were the only occupants, confirming Ty's comment that this was probably the last car going up for the day.

The view from the top was well worth the trip up. "This really is the top, now—you're sure?" she teased Ty.

"I'm sure." Ty paused to exchange a few words of German with the cable-car operator. "He says to take our time, we've got fifteen minutes to look around before he's going back down."

"Since that's the last car going down, we don't want to miss him."

"Don't worry, we won't miss him." Ty carefully led her around the cable-car station so that she could get a better view. The narrow path had been cleared of snow. "What do you think?"

"I think . . ." Mary Ellen's enthusiastic reply trailed off midstream at the sight of their cable car, the *last* cable car, descending without them! ". . . we're in trouble!"

CHAPTER TEN

"Our employer will be pleased." Pierre made the proud announcement to Josef. "Here, look for yourself." Pierre handed the pair of high-powered binoculars to Josef.

"All I see is a cable car."

"That's right. The last cable car down from the top of the mountain, and Stevenson and the woman aren't on it."

"I feel guilty leaving the woman up there as well," Josef confessed. "Do you think she will be all right?"

"You are getting soft in your old age," Pierre reprimanded him.

"It is not a matter of getting soft or getting old," Josef denied. "I do not like involving women or children in my work."

"Stop worrying." Pierre grinned lasciviously. "She has Stevenson to keep her warm."

"I still don't like it. When we took this job, you said nothing about a woman being involved."

"It was as big a surprise to me as it was to you," Pierre maintained with self-righteous indignation.

Recognizing the signs of an imminent temper tantrum, Josef tried placating Pierre with a compliment. "It was a good plan."

Since it was his plan, Pierre naturally agreed. "It was a brilliant plan!"

"Tell me again how you arranged it," Josef requested.

"It was simple, but then brilliant plans often are. You remember that I told you our employer said we should step up our surveillance and harass Stevenson?"

"I remember. But how did you know Stevenson would be coming up here? The rest of the tour didn't come."

"I didn't know he was coming up here. I kept my eyes open and my brain operating. You should try it some time," Pierre told Josef, in the manner of a master offering advice to an apprentice. "Now, as I was saying, I got my brilliant idea the moment I realized Stevenson intended going all the way up on the last cable car. Foolish error on his part, but then he never had a chance against a pro like me. And you," Pierre added as Josef glared at him.

"How did you get that operator to agree to leave them up on the mountain?"

Pierre rubbed his fingers together. "I made it worth his while."

"Who paid for it? Does that come out of our cut?"

Pierre frowned at Josef's practicality. "Those are details we take care of later. The main thing is that the plan worked, just as I said it would."

"What do we do now?" Josef asked.

"We go back down to Innsbruck and enjoy a nice dinner with a bottle of wine to celebrate."

Josef doubted that he'd be able to eat much knowing he'd left a woman marooned on top of that mountain. The bottle of wine sounded good to him, though. He just might consume it all himself; perhaps then he could forget what they'd done. Josef snatched one last regretful look at the mountain peak before following Pierre.

On top of that mountain peak Mary Ellen was still shouting and frantically waving her hands at the tiny image of the cable car as it slipped from view. "Come back here! You can't leave us up here!"

"Marielle, it's no use. You're only going to shout yourself hoarse."

She turned to Ty and said, "What are we going to do?" with such helplessness that he swore under his breath.

"Calm down and come here." He took her in

his arms and gave her a reassuring hug. "We'll be all right."

Over her head Ty was staring down the mountainside. His eyes were dark with a dangerous fury as he silently vowed retribution against the man who'd marooned them up here. But his immediate concern was for Mary Ellen's safety and well-being.

He eased her away from him. "Come on, let's go back around to the front of the station and see what's going on."

"You saw what's going on. That jerk left without us! And we weren't even gone five minutes of the fifteen-minute time limit he gave us! Ty, why would he leave like that?"

"I don't know. Maybe there was an emergency, maybe that wasn't the last car down."

"And maybe we really are stuck up here. Then what do we do?"

"We take it one step at a time, starting now."

They checked the cable-car station and found it tightly locked up. Just to make sure that no one was still inside, Ty pounded on the door while Mary Ellen peered through the windows.

"Nothing. There's no one in there, Ty."

"I'm afraid you're right." Hitting his fists against the door had helped to relieve some of the pent-up anger and frustration he was experiencing, but he was still a long way from being resigned to their plight.

"And since they locked the place up, it

doesn't look like there will be another cable car coming up tonight, does there?"

"It doesn't look that way, no," he had to agree. "But we still have several options open to us."

"Such as?"

"Such as I break into the station and borrow that pair of skis leaning in the corner and I ski down to the lower station and get help."

"What if that station is closed too? It will be dark soon and you'll be stuck down there somewhere on the mountainside. No, we can't separate." The thought of Ty out there, in the dark, alone and at the mercy of the elements, made her shiver.

Concerned, Ty made her sit down beside the station on a wooden bench which caught and retained some heat from the soon-to-be-setting sun. "Here, sit down before you fall down."

She saw that he was still eyeing the pair of skis through the window and the possibility that he might do something risky frightened her more than being marooned did. "Don't leave me up here. Promise me you'll stay with me."

The intensity of her voice matched the expression in her eyes. It was a look Ty couldn't refuse. "I'll stay."

Ty was reviewing their other options when he heard the unexpected sound of approaching footsteps. Immediately he launched into action, motioning Mary Ellen back against the station wall, where she'd be out of sight, and out of danger should any arise. Ty had no idea who was coming, but it could hardly be someone just passing by. Not on top of a seven-thousand-foot-high mountain peak.

Whatever he was expecting, it wasn't the sight of two old, weather-beaten men ambling along as if they were out for a leisurely walk. Both men wore the traditional Alpine attire of green loden cloth coats and knickers. Their feet were encased in thick wool socks and high, sturdy boots. On their heads each wore a hat, and the lower half of their faces was covered with shaggy white beards.

When Ty called out a greeting they replied in a dialect so thick that Ty could only understand every third word.

"Who are they?" Mary Ellen asked him.

Ty broke off his conversation with the two men to glare at her. "I thought I told you to stay put." The men looked harmless enough, but he didn't approve of Mary Ellen's disobeying his orders.

She was unimpressed by his anger. "Don't yell at me. Who are they?"

"I'm still trying to find that out. I think they're saying that they're goatherds."

Mary Ellen stuck her hands in her sweater pockets and shivered. "Isn't it a little cold up here for goats?"

"It's cold up here for people too." He'd already lent her his jacket but she'd adamantly refused to accept it, saying her sweater was warm enough.

"Does that mean you don't think they are goatherds?"

"I'm not sure yet." Ty went on to question the two men about the cable car. As he'd feared, they confirmed that the last car had gone down and none would be coming back up until tomorrow morning at eight. They also said that it was not the first time someone had missed the last cable car.

While Ty was engaging the two men in conversation he couldn't help but notice the lecherous looks the self-proclaimed goatherds kept giving Mary Ellen. It came as no surprise to hear them eagerly offer Mary Ellen shelter in their hut. They carefully explained that regrettably there wouldn't be room for Ty as well. The hut was small, very small.

"What are they saying?" Mary Ellen asked Ty.

"They've offered to let you stay in their hut, which is supposed to be somewhere nearby."

"How nice of them." Mary Ellen smiled at the two men.

The goatherds almost smacked their lips in appreciation and anticipation.

"I don't think being nice had anything to do with it," Ty told her. "They invited you. Only you."

The smile left her face. "You're kidding."

"No."

Horrified, she stepped behind Ty for protection. "But they each look old enough to be my grandfather."

"They do, don't they? That doesn't seem to have slowed them down, however."

"Great. We're marooned on top of a mountain with a pair of dirty old men! I hope you told them no."

Ty grinned sardonically. "I told them that you're my woman and I wouldn't trust two such obviously virile men to stay alone with my woman."

"That was laying it on a bit thick."

"So long as it works."

It did work. The two goatherds grumbled a bit, but when they saw Ty had no intention of letting Mary Ellen leave his side, they finally included Ty in their invitation.

The two goatherds, who'd introduced themselves as Fritz and Ernst, hadn't been exaggerating when they'd said their hut was small. But at least it was shelter for the night and it did have a fireplace and a generous supply of firewood. Fritz and Ernst generously shared their evening meal—thick dark bread, cheese, and chunks of ham. In turn Mary Ellen shared the large bar of chocolate she'd bought earlier in Munich.

The fire heated the room to a toasty temperature. Mary Ellen's eyes were drooping sleepily when she heard one word she understood out of all the German she didn't. Suddenly she was wide awake. "Avalanche?"

"Take it easy," Ty murmured, tightening the arm he'd kept around her shoulders since the moment they'd walked into the mountain hut.

He wouldn't put it past Ernst or Fritz to try and sneak a pinch or two the moment his back was turned, so he kept Mary Ellen close to avoid trouble. "We were talking about—"

"Avalanches. I know, I understood that part."

He gently tugged on her hair in reprimand for interrupting him. "We were talking about the fact that there wasn't as much snow this last winter as there has been in past years, which means there isn't much danger of avalanches."

"Isn't much danger, but some. And I was yelling!" Her exclamation was whispered.

"Forget it. After all, we're practically perched on top of the mountain here, there's nothing above us."

Fritz and Ernst claimed Ty's attention with another lengthy declaration in German.

"Now what are they talking about?" she asked Ty.

"I think they're telling me dirty jokes. I only hope I'm laughing in the appropriate places. My knowledge of German doesn't cover bawdy-joke telling."

"Funny, I would have thought that a man with your extensive experience would be a pro at deciphering off-color humor."

"If that's what you think, then I fear you have a totally false impression of my life-style, Marielle."

"Really?"

"Yes, really. I may have sown a few wild oats in my time—"

"A few?" she challenged him.

"All right, a lot—but that doesn't mean that I haven't settled down with age."

"You? Settle down? Never. Not even when you're as old as Ernst and Fritz here."

Once again Mary Ellen had thrown Ty for a loop. He didn't like the fact that Mary Ellen thought him incapable of settling down. Granted he and commitment had never gotten along in the past, but that didn't mean a man couldn't change. Not that he had changed yet, but he might in the future. She could at least have given him the benefit of a doubt, and not stated her opinion with such utter conviction.

Ty was so involved with his own jumbled thoughts, he was unaware that Fritz had poured Mary Ellen a glass of schnapps or that she'd accepted it and drunk it.

The alcohol burned all the way down Mary Ellen's throat. It did warm her up. Immediately. So much so that she peeled off her sweater.

Her action temporarily displaced Ty's arm from her shoulders and gained his attention. "What are you doing?"

"It's hot in here."

Ty viewed her flushed face with alarm. Was she ill? He laid his hand on her forehead. She didn't feel feverish, but she looked it. Her eyes were bright, her breathing fast. Then he noticed the empty glass in her hand. "What did you drink?"

As quickly as Ty took the first glass out of her hand, Fritz replaced it with another. Mary Ellen downed the contents in one gulp. The second glassful went down smoother than the first.

"Give me that." Ty angrily grabbed the second empty glass away from her and rapped out a command to Fritz and Ernst in German.

The two old men were laughing uproariously, patting each other on the back and jabbing each other with their elbows—carrying on like a pair of schoolboys.

Aggravated, Ty turned away from them. "Mary Ellen, you're not to drink any more, do you hear me?"

"I hear—*hiccup*—you. And I see you." She blinked at him myopically. "Two of you. I didn't know you were twins."

Ty clenched his jaw and muttered under his breath. Schnapps was potent stuff, especially at this high altitude, where the alcohol entered the bloodstream faster. Of course Fritz and Ernst denied having any coffee in their small store of supplies, so Ty had no means of sobering her up.

Hoping to distract the two men from causing any further trouble, Ty reached for a deck of cards he'd spotted earlier and showed Ernst and Fritz a few flashy card tricks. The men were impressed and demanded that Ty show them how he did it.

Watching him shuffling the cards Mary Ellen was fascinated by Ty's hands. He had long and narrow fingers that were faster than the eye as he performed the card trick. She had no trouble imagining those fingers gripping the steering wheel of a race car, or caressing the curves of a woman. The problem was that he'd no doubt caressed the curves of too many women. She frowned. He was too good with his hands.

"Did you cheat?" she demanded out of the blue.

"I beg your pardon?"

"When we played strip poker. Did you cheat?"

"What are you talking about?"

"Strip poker."

"Are you talking about the time—"

"When I was eighteen, yes. Did you cheat?"

"No. I didn't have to. Poker is not your game. Your eyes are too expressive."

Mary Ellen blinked. "They are?"

Ty nodded.

She melted against him and whispered in his ear. "Wanna hear a secret?"

He groaned as she swirled her tongue over his ear.

She took that to mean yes. "Ever since I was fifteen I've loved your eyes."

"That's nice." Ty's voice sounded strained.

"No, they're not nice. They're naughty. Naughty eyes, and sexy." She leaned back and studied his eyes, running her finger along his eyebrow. "I used to spend hours trying to describe them in my diary: chocolate eyes, mocha eyes, molasses eyes, maple-syrup eyes." She paused a moment to think. "You know, that's a lot of food. I must have been a hungry teenager."

"Marielle, this is fascinating. But—"

She repeated his last word and said, "I like that part of you too." Her hand dropped to his waist, around to the small of his back and down. . . .

Ty was getting desperate. Ernst and Fritz were busy practicing their newly learned card skills, but Ty doubted that would keep them occupied for long. And the communal, one-room mountain hut was not the place to finish what Mary Ellen was so temptingly starting. He had to bring her to her senses fast, before he lost his!

Hoping to shock her out of her amorous mood, he yanked her closer and kissed her. The plan backfired. Instead of resisting or protesting she responded so heatedly that Ty almost blew a fuse. Her tongue engaged his in an undulating battle that was as intoxicating as it was exciting.

The sound of Fritz and Ernst's laughing brought him back to reality. Sure enough, as soon as he opened his eyes he saw the two goatherds leaning forward in their chairs; a rapt audience. Ty was damned if he was going to provide erotic entertainment for a pair of old lechers!

Firmly setting Mary Ellen away from him Ty

issued her a stern but husky command: "Behave yourself!"

His anger served to squelch any further advances on Mary Ellen's part. However she couldn't resist cuddling up to him later that night as they shared a mat on the floor in front of the fireplace. A thick down comforter covered them and helped keep out the pervading cold.

Unable to bear her provocative wriggling another second, Ty clamped her to him and ordered, "Don't move."

"What's wrong?" Her question was mumbled against his throat.

"What you're doing would try the patience of a saint, and I'm no saint."

"I can tell." The words came out in a soft murmur.

Ty relieved his frustration by telling her exactly what he was going to do to her as soon as they were off this damn mountain and alone. He told her in graphic, erotic detail, listing in chronological order precisely where and how he was going to touch her. He didn't know whether to be insulted or relieved when Mary Ellen fell asleep midway through his recitation.

The first thing Mary Ellen was aware of the next morning was her head. It was also the second, third, and fourth thing. Instinctively she knew that even groaning would be painful. Ty took one look at her and then went in search of coffee. He didn't believe that Fritz and Ernst had told the truth last night when they'd denied possessing any. Sure enough, he easily found a box of instant-coffee packets. He built up the fire and soon had a pan of water boiling.

Mary Ellen grimaced at drinking the coffee black; she'd never been much of a coffee drinker and never took it black.

"Drink it. You need the caffeine."

She groaned. "I feel awful."

"I have seen you look better too," Ty agreed.

The lack of shower or bath facilities further lowered Mary Ellen's spirits. She didn't even have a toothbrush and her mouth felt as if the Prussian Army had marched through it.

Fritz and Ernst brought a blast of cold air in with them as they entered the hut. Apparently they'd been out collecting more firewood. Fritz offered Ty and Mary Ellen more black bread and cheese for breakfast, but they politely declined. They did accept the two wool blankets Ernst offered and followed his advice of wrapping the blankets around themselves to stay warm during the walk back to the cable-car station.

Ty and a hung-over Mary Ellen were ready and waiting when the cable car arrived. The operator, one they'd never seen before, looked stunned to see them and was completely at a loss as to how to handle the situation.

Ty was furious and showed no pity for the cable-car operator. He interrogated the man in terse German, demanding an explanation for such gross incompetence. The operator didn't have one. All he knew was that the man who'd operated the last car yesterday had not reported for work today. No one knew of his whereabouts.

"Ty, we don't have time to argue about it now. Our bus will be leaving Innsbruck in an hour, and we've got to be on it."

It went against the grain for him to leave the situation unresolved, but Ty realized that as far as Mary Ellen was concerned, getting off the mountain and catching that tour bus took precedence over bringing an official complaint against the operator who'd left them. Under the circumstances Ty decided not to press the issue but he did make a point of speaking to the supervisor once they reached the base cable car station and was promised a thorough investigation into the matter.

Any hopes Mary Ellen might have about being able to clean up in their hotel room were dashed by the sight of the tour bus, engine idling, parked in front of the hotel. As they stepped out of the taxi that had taken them from the cogwheel-railway terminus to the hotel, Bertha was standing on the curb waiting for them.

"You're late!" She glared at a point in the middle of Mary Ellen's forehead.

"We were stuck on top of a mountain all night."

"I don't care what your excuse is," Bertha retorted without even bothering to listen to what Mary Ellen had said.

180

"Bertha." Ty approached her and draped an arm around the tour guide's hefty shoulders. "A little word of friendly advice—if you value your job, then stow the reprimands! We don't expect the impossible, like concern or human kindness, but we do insist on courtesy. Understand?"

Eyes wide, Bertha nodded.

"Good." Ty released her. Smiling sardonically he gestured her on ahead of them. "Then let's all join the others on the bus and get moving, shall we? I've seen enough of Innsbruck to last me for a long while."

CHAPTER ELEVEN

"We were so worried about you," Irma exclaimed as Ty and Mary Ellen wearily took their seats on the bus. "We were going to invite you to join us for dinner last night, but they told us at the hotel that you'd never picked up your room key. What happened? Are you both all right?"

Ty and Mary Ellen both nodded, she more cautiously than he.

Irma gave them a moment to settle in. "Now can you tell us what happened?"

Ty briefly gave the retired couple a condensed version of their night's misadventures up on the mountain.

"You poor dears," Irma murmured.

Hearing Ty referred to as a "dear" made

Mary Ellen smile. She'd swallowed two aspirins with the help of a few sips from Irma's bottle of mineral water, and the pills had served to dull her headache. The scenery they were driving past made it difficult to stay in the doldrums. However Mary Ellen did make a point of keeping her eyes on the pastoral beauty of the Alpine valleys, and she avoided looking up at the snowy peaks.

The group stopped for lunch in Vaduz, the capital city of the tiny principality of Liechtenstein. Mary Ellen's first priority was to slip into the restaurant's ladies' room and freshen up. While it finally felt good to exchange the blouse and cardigan she'd slept in for a clean sweater from her tote bag, she wouldn't feel really comfortable until she'd had a hot shower.

Ty stood waiting for her in the foyer, and Mary Ellen observed that he had weathered the night better than she. Although he still hadn't had an opportunity to shave, the shadowy stubble darkening his face only added the adjective *untamed* to his adventuring good looks. The rebellious curl in his brown hair was also more apparent. His rangy figure was outwardly at ease, but Mary Ellen noticed the silent watchfulness in his eyes.

"Everything okay?" she asked as she joined him.

"Yeah."

Before Mary Ellen could question him further they were joined by several other members of the tour group.

"Where are Hank and Archie?" Irma asked. Ty and Mary Ellen's disappearance made Irma worry that someone else might get lost, marooned, or whatever.

"Hank took Archie to the post office," Viola answered.

"To mail him back to the States?" Sheldon teasingly suggested.

Viola grinned. "No, to purchase some stamps for Archie's stamp collection. They said they'd meet us back at the bus."

They did, and the bus left Vaduz on time. It didn't take long to drive to Zurich. Their hotel was centrally located and their room thankfully possessed a shower. The first thing Mary Ellen did, before even unpacking, was to strip off her clothes, step under the cascade of warm water, and wash her hair.

She was soon feeling more like her old self again. Dressed in clean clothes she emerged from the bathroom and found Ty stretched out on their bed sound asleep. She experienced a vague sense of guilt. If her flashes of memory were correct, then she was no doubt the one responsible for having given him a sleepless night last night.

Smiling down at Ty she silently promised to make it up to him. The first step in doing that would be to check out the decadent dream of a dress she'd seen in the window of a small shopping arcade next to the hotel. Tonight was the visit to the casino, and she was looking forward to an elegant night out. She was also looking

184

forward to seeing Ty's face when he saw her in that dress. She'd just written him a note saying she'd gone shopping with Viola, and was just about to leave the room when the phone rang.

Mary Ellen quickly answered it, but the ringing had awakened Ty.

"This is Bertha speaking. I am calling to inform you that the casino tour this evening has been canceled."

"Canceled!" Mary Ellen was dismayed. "But why?"

"It has been replaced with a visit to a lively nightclub for a taste of Zurich's night life." Bertha sounded as if she were reading the words from a travel brochure.

"I don't want to go to a nightclub," Mary Ellen declared.

"It is an excellent club," Bertha stated. "My brother-in-law runs it, so I should know."

Mary Ellen was not impressed. "Why was the visit to the casino canceled?"

Bertha mumbled something that Mary Ellen asked her to repeat.

"There is no casino in Zurich!" Bertha practically shouted.

"No casino?"

"That's right. Are you joining us at the nightclub or not?"

"Not."

"What about Mr. Stevenson?"

"Ask him yourself." Mary Ellen handed over the phone to Ty.

"What's wrong?" he asked her, ignoring the receiver he held in his hand.

"Bertha just canceled the casino tour. She claims there's no casino in Zurich. Do you believe it? How could she not know that beforehand? How come you didn't know that?"

"Marielle, despite what you might think, I do not have a memorized list of every casino in Europe."

"And Bertha?"

"I doubt if she has a memorized list either."

"I doubt if she has a memory, period."

Ty briefly spoke to Bertha and turned down her invitation to the nightclub.

"This is the final substitution for the 'Heidelberg By Night' tour," she warned him.

"I certainly hope so. It's about time that poor Heidelberg tour was put to rest," he said right before hanging up.

Ty focused his attention on Mary Ellen. "Hey, cheer up," he softly requested.

She sighed, not just a dainty exhalation but a bona fide, hearty sigh. "I was really looking forward to going out to a casino tonight. I've never been to one, you know."

"No problem. If you want to go to a casino, I'll take you."

"Ty, didn't you hear what I told you? Bertha said that there aren't any casinos in Zurich."

"She's probably right. But there is a casino only a short drive away from here," he told her. "It's across the border in Germany, so you'd have to bring your passport."

"I thought you said you didn't have a memorized list of all the casinos in Europe."

"I don't. I just happen to know about the one near Lake Constance."

"What are you suggesting?"

"That I rent a car and take you out for a night on the town. It may not be this town, but it will be a night out. What do you say?" he asked her. "Are you game?"

"Absolutely!"

"No aftereffects from your hangover this morning?"

"No, I'm feeling a lot better now. I'm glad I decided to take it easy for a while instead of going right out exploring, but I would like to go down to one of the stores next door and do a little exploring now. Viola's invited me to go with her."

"Go ahead. I'm going to stay up here and make a few phone calls." Ty wanted to check in with Lars to see what the latest scuttlebutt was concerning Mr. Q. He also needed to touch base with his parents for the latest on his father's health. And then there was his sister Jennifer in London, who had already threatened to call the cavalry if he didn't keep in touch.

Mary Ellen gulped when she converted the price of the dream dress from Swiss francs to American dollars. She might not have had the nerve to try it on if it hadn't been for Viola's prodding.

"Go on. If you're not meant to have the dress, it won't fit."

It did fit. Like a glove. And once she got it on, the price was irrelevant. The champagne-colored satin gown had a strapless bodice that molded her breasts and a stiff bouffant skirt that ended just above her knees. The color was perfect on her. Viola told her so, and the saleswoman told her so as she wrote out a receipt.

When Mary Ellen explained that it was for a very special evening out, the woman beamed and nodded understandingly. "Is there anything else you need?"

"A shawl, perhaps?" Viola suggested.

Mary Ellen nodded. Her raincoat would definitely ruin the elegant image she was trying to project with this dress.

The store had just the thing, a shawl made of hand-crocheted mohair yarn; lightweight yet warm. It was so lovely that Viola picked up one to add to her purchase, a lovely silk dress she hoped would impress Hank.

"I'll have this one," Mary Ellen said, fingering a black mohair shawl. "One more thing. . . ."

"Shoes, perhaps?" the saleslady asked, pictures of an even larger sale forming in her head.

"No. But is there a hair salon nearby that you could recommend?" She wanted a special look for the special evening.

The saleswoman directed her next door. Mary Ellen left the beauty shop an hour later, feeling and looking like a new woman. Viola felt the same way.

"I hope Hank likes this new style," Viola murmured.

"You look great," Mary Ellen reassured her. "Hank doesn't stand a chance!"

Viola returned the compliment. "Neither does Ty."

"I want to surprise him tonight."

"I'm sure you will."

"I don't want him sneaking any peeks until I'm ready."

"You're welcome to use my room to change in if you want," Viola offered.

"If you don't mind, I think I'll just use your phone and see if Ty's still in our room. He mentioned something about renting a car. Maybe he's already gone out to do that."

Ty was just on his way out when Mary Ellen called him. "Where are you?" he demanded. "I was just coming to look for you."

"I'm in Viola's room. Our shopping spree took longer than we'd expected."

"Souvenir shopping again, I suppose."

Mary Ellen grinned and murmured a noncommittal reply.

"Listen, now that you're back I'm going to go out and pick up the rental car. It should only take me about half an hour or so."

"Fine. I'll see you then."

"Marielle . . ."

"Yes?"

"I hope you haven't forgotten all the post-casino activities we have planned. I believe I outlined a few of the high points last night before you fell asleep."

"I haven't forgotten a thing," she said in a husky whisper.

"Good."

"It will be," she promised him.

Mary Ellen returned to their room to dress and put on her makeup. The hair designer had applied a highlighting mousse that increased the shine in the streaks of gold in her light-brown hair. Left loose as it was, the extravagantly curly style added a wanton wildness to her appearance. Shimmering gold eye shadow and nail polish, newly purchased, provided the finishing touch. The only jewelry she wore was a gold chain around her neck.

"What are you doing in there?" Ty had returned and been dressed and waiting for half an hour. "You've been in there for ages. Come on, we've got to get a move on."

"Close your eyes." She opened the bathroom door. "And don't peek," she added as she saw his left eyelid move suspiciously. She glided into the room. "Okay, now look."

Ty opened his eyes.

"Well, what do you think?"

He didn't say a word, he just looked at her in a way that made her toes curl.

"Do you like the dress?"

"I always knew you were beautiful, but I'm not sure I want everyone else knowing exactly how beautiful." His voice was dark and sensual.

Mary Ellen frowned down at the expanse of

bare skin revealed by the dress's strapless bodice. "You think it's too revealing?"

"I think it's perfect." His hand gently cupped her cheek as he added, "And so are you."

She shifted his hand to her mouth and kissed his fingers. "You don't look so bad yourself, sir."

Ty was wearing a tuxedo that had obviously been personally tailored to fit his lean body. The crisp white shirt provided a dramatic contrast to his tanned face. The formal clothing intensified the intangible aura of strength and authority he possessed.

His silk bow tie, however, was ever so slightly askew, a small testimony to the fact that here was a man who would conform only so far and then propriety could take a hike. The devil-may-care gleam in his dark eyes and the rakish tilt of his eyebrows reaffirmed it: here was a man who did things his own way, and did them well.

One of the things he did well was drive a car. And what a car it was. A Ferrari, he proudly told her. She was sure he couldn't have rented it from Hertz.

By the time she gathered enough breath to request that Ty slow down, her gold-tinted nails had left their half-moon shape in her palms and her heart felt permanently lodged in her throat.

"Relax," he told her. "I do this for a living, remember?"

"I know you're an excellent driver but all

191

those other drivers out there may be rotten. And I'd just as soon we didn't cross paths with them."

Ty did ease up on the accelerator then. "It feels so good to be behind the wheel again."

Mary Ellen felt a stab of pain. Soon Ty would be back in the world of racing, and she in the world of fund raising. But until then she vowed to make the most of the time they had left together.

To Mary Ellen's awed eyes the large casino with its high ceilings and ornate chandeliers looked like a palace. A number of the men were in tuxedos. The women in expensive gowns made Mary Ellen glad she'd left her raincoat back at the hotel. So her mohair shawl wasn't mink and she wasn't dripping in diamonds. Wearing this dress and walking in with Ty at her side made her feel like the most beautiful woman present.

"Where would you like to start?" Ty asked her.

Mary Ellen only saw one thing she recognized. "The roulette table."

Ty insisted on purchasing the special roulette chips for her. He then proceeded to explain the game's rules and procedures, which bets were fatal, which were shrewd. Mary Ellen then proceeded to ignore all of his advice by randomly placing her chip on the red six.

The hum of the spinning ivory ball as it circled the rotating wheel seemed inordinately loud to Mary Ellen's nervous ears. She held her

192

breath at the soft ping as the ball finally dropped into a numbered pocket. She closed her eyes as those around her *oohed* and *aahed* at her having placed the right bet.

"Marielle, you won."

"What?" Her eyes sprung open. Sure enough the ball was in the pocket with a red number six. "I won?"

"You won."

She threw her arms around his neck. "I can't believe it!"

As the night wore on, Ty was the one who couldn't believe it. Mary Ellen disproved every theory on the laws of statistical probability. She didn't follow any logical course of action, but she kept on winning anyway. It didn't take long for others to cotton on to her winning streak and to follow her random betting strategy, if it could be called strategy. She called it intuition. He called it strange.

Whatever it was, it got out of hand as the evening wore on.

"Mary Ellen, I think you should quit now while you're ahead."

"Quit?" Her cheeks were flushed, her eyes bright. "But I'm on a winning streak!"

The croupier eyed her and asked if she wanted sex.

She haughtily returned his stare. "I beg your pardon?"

"Not s-e-x. It's s-e-c-h-s," Ty softly informed her, "and it's German for the number six."

"Oh. Yes, keep it there."

Ty decided to use his own secret weapons to combat Mary Ellen's obvious case of gambling fever. Whenever she leaned over to place a bet, he leaned right behind her. He was her seductive shadow. His presence was meant to distract her, and it did. Especially when he slipped his fingers beneath her shawl and ran them across her shoulder blades. The strapless design of her dress left her very vulnerable to the kind of caresses Ty was bestowing upon her.

She turned to remind him of their public surroundings, but the words were forgotten the moment her eyes met his. The undisguised desire she saw reflected there worked its magic on her. He was looking at her in that special way again, the way that made her feel as if she were burning up inside.

"Remember, the *real* excitement begins when this is over and you and I are alone," he told her in a deeply sexy voice.

She couldn't resist flirting with him. "More betting?"

"No." His eyes slowly toured her body, visually peeling every article of clothing away from her. "This will be a sure thing."

Even though Mary Ellen continued to play the game of roulette, her concentration was no longer entirely on the spinning wheel. How could it be, when the very air between herself and Ty was heavy with sensuality? Every move he made, every word he whispered, was intended to heighten her anticipation.

Distracted though she was, Mary Ellen kept on winning. When Ty practically swept Mary Ellen away from the table, the crowd complained, distressed at losing their lucky forecaster. To ensure that Mary Ellen didn't complain, too, Ty kissed her.

"Where are we going?" she mumbled against his lips in between nibbles.

"To celebrate. In private."

To her surprise, after cashing in her chips Ty didn't take her to the Ferrari parked outside. Instead he led her through a doorway and up a flight of stairs to the casino's private guest rooms. He kept her distracted by whispering intimate promises in her ear as they made their way along the hallway.

"This is it." Ty stopped in front of a door and pulled a key out of his tuxedo jacket pocket.

"Ty, we've got a room in Zurich.."

"Which will still be there when we return to Zurich tomorrow morning. The tour stays in Zurich for two days, so there's no hurry, is there?"

"No." She followed him inside. "No hurry."

"We're going to take this very slowly, right?"

"Mmmm, right."

Saying it was one thing, sticking to it was something else. Their minds may have said, *Slow,* but their bodies were chanting, *Fast.*

"You'll have to show me your unbeatable gambling system," he told her while he kissed his way from her earlobe to her collarbone.

195

"I don't keep it there." She gasped as his hands slid around her waist to tease her ribs.

"No?"

"No." She shifted against him. "Try a little to your left."

The movement put the palms of his hands directly over her breasts. The satin material of her dress only served to intensify the caress, its slippery texture sliding over her skin and his.

"This dress is fantastic," he growled, "but how do I get you out of it?"

"Very carefully."

"Very funny."

"I'll give you a hint." She guided his hand over to the small side zipper, the cornerstone to the dress's form-fitting construction. "Start here."

He did, with excellent results. The dress proved to be extremely cooperative. So was Mary Ellen.

Once her dress was safely deposited on a nearby chair, she was free to tease temptingly the corners of his mouth with her tongue while her fingers undid his bow tie and slid it out from beneath the starched collar of his dress shirt. Ty shrugged out of his jacket and helped her in her quest to unfasten the studs on his shirt. Soon it, too, joined his jacket.

Smiling seductively Mary Ellen stepped away from him and kicked off her high-heeled shoes. Ty ducked as one of the shoes accidentally flew in his direction. "Getting feisty, are we?" The devilish gleam in his eyes warned her that he was up to no good.

"It was an accident."

"Sure it was." He slid out of his shoes and socks and proceeded to stalk her.

Mary Ellen was easy to catch, because she was distracted by the sight of him. Wearing only a pair of elegantly tailored black pants, he was bare chested and barefoot. He was also eyeing her with that special look that made her melt.

She was wearing much less than he. Her strapless underwire bra had been a last-minute purchase. As were the pure silk French panties with the lacy edges.

She shrieked as Ty grabbed her and began tickling her. "I've got you now!" In a rumbling voice he ordered her up against the wall.

"The wall?" she repeated in the middle of a giggle.

"That's right. No arguing."

"Who's arguing?" Laughter made her sides ache. Hunger for Ty made the rest of her ache.

"All right, now face the wall and spread out your hands," he instructed her. "No, not like that. Put your hands on the wall."

"So you can tickle me again. Forget it."

"I won't tickle you. I promise. Put your hands on the wall. Over your head."

"You promise you won't tickle me?"

"Promise. May my gas tank be filled with sugar should I lie."

Recognizing the vow from their teenage

years she put her hands on the wall. "Hey, this is carpeted."

"Marielle, I didn't set this up for you to notice the decorating."

"And you didn't set this up to tickle me either," she reminded him, just in case.

"That's right." His words vibrated against her ear as he moved in behind her. "I set this up so that I can frisk you in hopes of discovering your secrets."

"What secrets?" Her voice was a husky whisper. "For winning at roulette?"

"*All* your secrets."

With that evocative promise Ty closed in. Her stance allowed him free access to the back fastening of her bra. He nuzzled the nape of her neck as he freed her from the piece of lingerie. Each move was slow and deliberate and left Mary Ellen feeling as if she were a very special present that he was taking great pleasure in unwrapping.

His nuzzling caresses moved from her neck to her throat, up over her jaw, to her ear. With one hand he smoothed her shoulder-length hair out of his way. Now that her ear was uncovered, he nibbled and tasted with his tongue while his free hand went in search of creamy skin also recently uncovered.

Mary Ellen's breath caught in her throat as she felt one warm finger mark a trail down the center of her body, from collarbone to navel and back again. She'd been expecting a more direct approach, but Ty was keeping to his word and taking things slowly. His leisurely loving was infinitely arousing.

When he finally took her breast in his hand and stroked her with his thumb, she was already trembling. Leaning her head back against his shoulder she could only close her eyes and enjoy.

But Ty had still more pleasures in store for her. Now both his hands worked their magic on her, until her flesh was firm and quivering. Only then did his caresses move down to flirt with the lacy edge of her silk panties. Eventually his skillful fingers slipped beneath the bit of silk to explore her most intimate secrets. The finesse of his movements enthralled her, the precision of his touch shattered her. All at once she was hurtling through space without a safety net.

"Ty!"

A smile of satisfaction curved his lips as he felt her tighten and then explode in his arms. He held her until she regained the ability to stand on her own.

Even then her knees still trembled and her body still felt weightless. "Illegal search and seizure!" she gasped.

"You give me seizures," he returned in a thick voice.

"Not yet I haven't, but I intend to." Moving faster than he'd expected Mary Ellen pivoted in his arms. Placing both hands on his bare shoulders she pushed him backward until he toppled onto the bed.

"You're overdressed for this occasion," she decided, and proceeded to unbuckle his slacks. Her nimble fingers deliberately stroked him as she undid the zipper. His response was immediate and unmistakable.

"Now it's my turn to frisk you," she purred.

He groaned with anticipation that grew into painful pleasure.

Mary Ellen was very thorough in her investigation, leaving no territory untouched. "I don't feel anything that shouldn't be there, but one can never be sure without a strip search."

She peeled away his black Jockey underwear and revealed him in all his glory. Thrilled by his masculine strength Mary Ellen shifted her position from beside him until she was perched atop his thighs. With a sensual boldness she'd never known she possessed, she eagerly guided him to her.

Ty filled her with erotic completeness. His words of encouragement were rough with excitement as he urged her into a rise-and-fall rhythm that increased their pleasure. Thanks to his expert tutelage, she soon mastered the art of withdrawal and possession.

Ecstasy drenched her senses. The look on Ty's face matched hers—eyes glazed with passion, face flushed—and watching his pleasure increased her own.

With one final surge of motion Ty initiated a sliding rush that sent them both out of this world and into another—a world filled with pulsating excitement.

While Ty and Mary Ellen slept in each other's arms, their pursuers were busy. Not far from the casino, Pierre hung up the phone in a public phone booth. He'd just reported in to their employer.

"Well?" Josef demanded. "What did he say? What should we do now?"

Pierre's eyes gleamed in the dark. "Time is running out. Now we get serious."

CHAPTER TWELVE

As Mary Ellen lay in Ty's arms early the next morning, she was very much aware of the bittersweet passage of time. No matter how much she wanted things to be different, she had to keep reminding herself that the magic they were sharing was only temporary. This time she wasn't going to lose sight of that fact—she couldn't afford to.

When Ty had left her before, she'd been desolate. Now she loved him even more than she had then. For her own self-protection she had to keep her feet on the ground.

The sound of Ty's voice broke her out of her melancholy reverie. "Marielle?" He touched her gently, tenderly. "What are you thinking about?"

"Nothing." Her lashes shielded her eyes from view.

He tipped up her chin with his index finger. "You looked awfully sad to be thinking about nothing."

"After a night such as we just shared how could I be sad?" she replied with a smile.

Ty wasn't completely convinced. "That's what I'd like to know."

"I'd like to know what we're going to do today." She sat up in bed and tucked the feather comforter under her arms.

"I've got a few things planned," he replied with a lazy grin.

"I hope the first one is going back to Zurich so I can change." She ruefully stared at her bare arms and then at the length of champagne-colored satin draped over the chair. "While I love my new dress, I don't think it's exactly suitable for sightseeing."

"It allowed me to see your sights quite nicely," he murmured while tugging the feather comforter much lower. His grin widened as he appreciated the view.

"I'm glad you noticed."

"Oh, I noticed, all right." He traced the enticing valley between her breasts. "But I don't want too many other people noticing, so I packed a bag with more appropriate clothing."

"For me?"

"For both of us. My tux would look a little conspicuous too."

Mary Ellen hugged him. "Thank you."

203

"Remembering how you are about washing your hair and brushing your teeth, I also packed your makeup bag."

That earned him another hug and a kiss, which led to more intimate caresses. Passion flared and it was another hour before they got out of bed.

"How much did I win last night?" Mary Ellen asked Ty as they shared the bathroom. She was brushing her hair and he was shaving.

"At the roulette table, you mean?" He grinned at her knowingly as she stuck her tongue out at him. When he told her the dollar amount of her winnings, she was stunned.

"That will pay for my new dress!"

"You know, even if it is the oldest casino game still in existence, most people do not win at roulette as easily as you did."

"Easily?" she repeated with feigned huffiness. "I'll have you know that I put a great deal of thought into choosing my bets."

"You didn't follow any of the advice I gave you."

"That's why I won," she couldn't resist pointing out.

Their teasing banter continued as they dressed. It wasn't until they were eating their breakfast of warm croissants and freshly brewed coffee that Mary Ellen remembered to ask Ty about the phone calls he'd made from Zurich the night before. "Did you call Jennifer?"

"Yes. I called Jennifer. Again." His sigh held

masculine impatience as he buttered another croissant. "I just called her from Copenhagen a couple days ago, I don't know why she gets so agitated."

"It might have something to do with the fact that you're being chased across Europe by a pair of thugs."

"Jennifer doesn't know anything about that," he retorted.

"She doesn't have to; she knows you. And she knows you're always in trouble."

"Me?" His expression was one of boyish innocence. "I'm just a regular stay-at-home kind of guy."

I wish you were, Mary Ellen found herself thinking. Then she might have some hope of him settling down and loving her. But there was no possibility of that. And, actually, she wouldn't want to change Ty. She just wished that he were less devil-may-care sometimes.

"There you go frowning again," he told her.

"I was trying to picture you in a pair of slippers, reading a paper in your easy chair."

"And?"

"And it didn't work. You weren't meant for domesticity."

"Why not?"

She shrugged, as if the matter wasn't of much importance. "I don't know why not. You're too wild to be corralled, I guess."

Ty was irked at being compared to some kind of unbroken stallion. If she thought him to be that unfettered, why didn't she at least make the effort to try and lasso him? Instead it sounded as if she'd given up on him.

"Now *you're* frowning," she told him. "What's wrong, were you trying to picture yourself in slippers too?"

"No."

He sounded curt and disgruntled. Mary Ellen blamed his mood on their teasing discussion of domesticity. Obviously he got impatient at even the most casual mention of the topic.

She quickly changed the subject. "How did Jennifer sound when you spoke to her?"

"The same as always," Ty answered. "I also called my parents."

"How's your father doing?"

"He's getting a bit stronger each day, but it takes time."

Ty failed to mention the third call he'd made, the one to Lars Nielsen in Copenhagen. Lars had given him the disturbing news that Mr. Q's two goons had gotten into some sort of trouble with the Danish authorities, but they'd been released and deported from the country. As for Mr. Q himself, he was still alive and madder than hell at Ty. Hopefully the card-sharp would get his own soon and Ty wouldn't have to worry about the ridiculous matter any longer.

Resolving to forget Mr. Q and his goons Ty focused his thoughts on the plans he'd made for the day. "This is the third Monday in April," he told Mary Ellen. "Do you know what that means?"

To her it meant that there were only four days left of her vacation, but she was sure it didn't mean the same to him, so she shook her head.

"It means that in Zurich they're celebrating."

"Celebrating what?" When he told her she looked at him with suspicion. "Sex-what?"

"Marielle, you seem to have a one-track mind," he chastised her with a devilish grin.

"Which means it's in German and means six-something, right?"

"Right. Sechseläuten. It's a spring festival celebrating the end of winter. At precisely six this evening Old Man Winter is burned in effigy, in case you're wondering where the number six fits in."

"You've been to this festival before?"

"Yes."

Mary Ellen wondered who he'd been with, then decided it was probably better that she didn't know.

Mary Ellen and Ty were back in Zurich well in time to check out the festivities. Their absence the night before had gone unnoticed because most of the rest of the tour group had been out until midnight themselves, visiting Bertha's brother-in-law's nightclub. From the brief conversation Mary Ellen had had with Irma, no one had been impressed.

"I was ready to leave at ten," Irma said, "but they refused to let anyone out. The people in our group were the only customers they had, and they weren't about to let us leave. How about you?" Irma asked her. "How did your night go?"

"Wonderfully."

Irma grinned and thankfully didn't ask for details.

"Are you going to watch the burning of the Böögg tonight?" Mitzi inquired as she joined them in the hotel lobby. "According to my guidebook it's part of the Sechseläuten celebration."

"Yes, Ty and I thought we'd go."

In the end a group of them went; Irma and Sheldon, Hank and Viola, Archie and Mitzi.

Mary Ellen wasn't sure when the feeling of being watched hit her, but it came sometime during the colorful parade they were all observing. In honor of the celebration the streets lining the parade route were decked out with flags. The participants wore the traditional and often elaborate costumes of their particular trade guild. A group of white-wigged men with tricornered white-plumed hats rode by on horseback, the silken banners they carried fluttering in the cold wind blowing over Lake Zurich.

Mary Ellen welcomed the warmth of her new mohair shawl, which she wore as a scarf tucked beneath her raincoat. But the shivers running up her spine were not caused by the chill in the air. They were caused by a sudden premonition of danger.

Before she could convey her fears to Ty, she

felt someone grab hold of her shoulder bag and pull. Mary Ellen cried out while fiercely fighting to retain possession of her bag.

Hearing her shout of alarm Ty turned to see what was the matter. He moved fast, faster than Pierre had anticipated. Pierre tried to pull back, but it was too late. By then Pierre had already initiated the shoving motion with which he'd intended to send Ty sprawling into the street. Unfortunately Ty was now out of reach and Pierre's shoving hands contacted with the back of a policeman and sent him sprawling instead.

Pierre didn't hang around to apologize to the official for his mistake. He simply vanished in the crowd, as did Josef, the would-be purse-snatcher.

Ty's first concern was for Mary Ellen. "Are you all right?" His hands gripped her arms.

"Yes. That man tried to take my purse!"

"What's going on?" Sheldon demanded. "Are you two okay?"

"We're fine. Someone tried to steal Mary Ellen's purse."

"Oh, my goodness!" Irma exclaimed.

"Did you deck him?" Archie wanted to know.

"No, he got away," Mary Ellen replied.

Archie shook his head regretfully. "Too bad."

"I'll bet that's how that policeman got knocked down," Irma volunteered.

"What policeman?" Ty asked her.

"The one that was pushed into the street a few feet from here. Luckily he wasn't hurt, but he was sure mad. I'll bet that policeman was knocked down by the purse snatcher as he was making his getaway. Maybe we should tell the policeman about it."

"I don't think that's necessary," Mary Ellen said. She didn't want to draw attention to herself and to Ty. Making a report of the attempted robbery would entail leaving their names with the police, which would only make it easier for the thugs following them to trail Ty. Against her better judgment Ty had already left his name with the cable-car authorities in Innsbruck.

As it turned out the issue became moot, since the policeman could no longer be found.

"Ty, do you think this was tied in with the men who are following you?" she asked him as they stood aside from the other tour members.

"It's unlikely. Did you get a look at the man?"

"No. I was too busy trying to keep hold of my purse. Sorry."

"Don't worry about it. Chances are that this was just a simple case of purse snatching. Someone probably saw the opportunity to make some money and went for it."

"I hope you're right."

"Listen, I think I'd better take you back to the hotel. You look pretty shaken."

"I'll be fine."

"Marielle . . ."

"No, really. I'm fine. And I don't want to miss the grand finale."

"All right," he eventually agreed. "But stick close to me." He put his arm around her waist and brought her nearer. She welcomed the security of his embrace and wished it could always be available to her.

If her smile seemed a little too broad, or her gaiety a bit too forced, no one seemed to notice. Zurich was alive with an infectious sense of merrymaking that invited everyone to join in the revelry. A viewing stand had been set up expressly to see the grand finale; the ceremonial burning of the Böögg, and they were all lucky enough to find seats.

"That huge stuffed snowman with the bow tie and the pipe is the Böögg?" Irma questioned. The figure was almost three times the height of a man and was perched on a platform atop a huge mound of straw.

"That's right," Ty confirmed. "He's meant to represent winter."

"He looks too cute to burn," Irma said.

Mary Ellen was inclined to agree with Irma.

"Listen, there are the church bells, ceremoniously ringing in spring." Viola's face was flushed with excitement.

Hank checked his watch. "It's six, right on the money."

"And, look, they're lighting the straw with torches!" Sheldon exclaimed while busily trying to capture everything on film.

The Böögg's burning at the stake was an

awesome sight. Through the smoke the mounted guildsmen rode, triumphantly galloping around the slowly diminishing, blazing figure atop the bonfire.

Several hundred feet away Pierre was glaring at Josef. "It isn't enough that you ruined my last plan by playing tug-of-war with that woman's purse instead of simply grabbing it? Now what is the matter?"

Josef sneezed three times before being able to answer. When he did his voice was raw and raspy. "There are horses here."

"So?"

Josef sneezed again. "I am terribly allergic to horses." He blew his nose. "You said they would be burning some snowman. You said nothing about more horses. Those horses at the parade have already set off my allergies. Look at my eyes, they are so swollen I can barely see."

Pierre swore and stamped his feet, partly to keep them warm. "All right, we will stop for today. There are too many people here anyway. But we must get Stevenson at the tour's next stop."

"Why does our employer want us to grab Stevenson now anyway?"

"Our instructions are to rough him up to teach him a lesson. That's why I had you distract the rest of the group by grabbing that woman's purse."

"What lesson?"

Pierre shrugged. "What do we care? We are getting paid to do a job and we will do it."

Josef continued sneezing. "I have to leave," he mumbled through his handkerchief.

Pierre followed more slowly. He jumped as the fireworks stuffed inside the Böögg caught fire and exploded. The crowd cheered at the huge *boom* that proclaimed to all of Zurich: *The Böögg is dead, spring has arrived!*

Pierre made a proclamation of his own. "Next time, Stevenson. We will get you the first time the bus stops tomorrow. You can count on that."

Pierre wasn't counting on the sheer absurdity of that first stop the next morning. "A cuckoo clock factory!"

"Maybe we should wait?" Josef suggested. They were both sitting in their car, which they'd parked down the road a bit from the factory's large parking lot that already contained three tour buses.

"No." Pierre's face hardened with determination. "We are running out of time! Our employer said that if we did not get the job done in the next twenty-four hours we would not receive the remainder of our payment for this job. We cannot afford to wait. We cannot afford to make any more mistakes."

"Do you have a plan?" Josef asked.

"The first thing we have to do is separate Stevenson from the rest of the tour."

Josef nodded. That sounded reasonable. "How do we do that?"

"Why must I do all the thinking?" Pierre flared. "Don't you ever get any ideas?"

"Perhaps it would be best to go inside and see what kind of inspiration strikes," Josef suggested.

Since there were several tour groups milling through the factory at once, it was not difficult for Pierre and Josef to attach themselves to one of them.

Josef listened to snatches of the pretty guide's speech. "Around 1730 Franz Ketterer had the extraordinary idea of using the call of the cuckoo bird to sound the striking of the hour. Perhaps he heard the alerting call of the bird in the Black Forest and thought to use it in his clocks. No one knows for sure."

Pierre ignored the guide's detailed speech about the history of the cuckoo clock and concentrated on devising a brilliant plan. Inspiration struck as they passed the area where the weights were stored. The pine-cone shapes were attached to the weight chains of the clocks.

"This is it!" Pierre exclaimed. "These would make excellent bolas."

"Excellent what?" Josef asked, completely stymied.

"Bolas—a weapon consisting of two heavy balls secured to the end of a strong cord. They are used by the Indians and gauchos of South America to entangle the legs of cattle."

"When were you ever in South America?" Josef demanded. His expression reflected his incredulity at Pierre's comment.

"Okay, so I've only read about it. But I'm sure these weights would work."

"I don't know. . . ."

"Do you have a better idea?"

"Not at the moment, no."

"Then shut up and let me concentrate."

By this time most of the people had left the mazelike workshop area and proceeded on to the main section of the building, the large showroom where cuckoo clocks were sold.

"You go on ahead and take a look at the clocks for sale," Ty told Mary Ellen. He could have sworn he'd seen Josef's tall figure towering over a group of tourists a few minutes ago, and he wanted to check it out. But first he wanted Mary Ellen out of the way.

Mary Ellen followed Ty's suggestion and joined Irma and Viola in the store.

Pierre and Josef, concealed behind a shipment of outgoing clocks, watched Ty retrace his steps. They stood immobile, waiting for their chance. It came when Ty stepped into a small anteroom that was off the main area.

As he entered the room Ty made a rapid assessment of his surroundings. Three of the room's walls were covered with cuckoo clocks, loudly ticking away. The fourth wall was taken up by a large window that looked out into the Black Forest. There were three possible routes of escape through three separate arched entryways. None of them had doors. For now the anteroom was empty, but he had a feeling it wouldn't stay that way for long. He was right.

Pierre's latest plan might have had a better chance for success had he omitted adding the last-minute gaucholike cry as he twirled the weights over his head and sent them flying through the air. Hearing Pierre's whoop, Ty dived for cover. The weights flew over Ty's head and shattered the plate glass window.

Pierre's second attempt knocked four cuckoos off their perch as they popped out to proclaim the hour.

There wasn't time for a third attempt.

"So much for getting serious," Josef muttered with a curse as clocks fell to the floor and shattered. In only a matter of seconds they would be surrounded by people coming to investigate the racket. "Now what do we do?"

"Run."

They did. They grabbed the first person through the door and shoved the hapless workman at Ty, preventing him from pursuing his attackers. Pierre and Josef scrambled over the windowsill and vaulted right on through the gaping embrasure. As they disappeared into the Black Forest, one damaged cuckoo emitted it's final forlorn *Kook-oooohhhh*.

CHAPTER THIRTEEN

Mary Ellen heard with a sense of dread the sound of glass shattering. Ty! For one brief moment fear held her frozen. Then there was more noise, a crashing cacophony, all coming from the factory section of the building. Mary Ellen tried to rejoin Ty back in the factory but found her way blocked by others.

"What a racket!" Sheldon exclaimed. "What do you think happened? One of the cuckoos get loose?"

"Mary Ellen, what's wrong?" Irma asked in concern. "You look about ready to faint."

"Ty stayed back there." Her words were disjointed and unsteady.

Irma misunderstood her concern. "You think he broke a couple of clocks? Accidents happen,

dear. I'm sure something can be worked out.
No need to get into a state about it."

Bertha's piercing voice could be heard over
the confusion. "Worldwind tour group, this
way! It's time to board the bus. Finish your
purchases and come along."

Mary Ellen freed herself from Irma's restraining hold and shoved her way to the fore-
front of the curious crowd. She had to know:
Was Ty all right? Instinct told her that he was
involved in some way with whatever had happened. She only prayed that it wasn't anything
too serious.

Frustrated by her inability to move faster
through the crowd, Mary Ellen cried out to
him. "Ty! Where are you?"

"Over here." His voice came from the midst
of the tightly knit group of people, officials
from the factory who reluctantly allowed her
through.

She was trembling by the time she reached
his side. Her eyes stung with the threat of tears
and her voice was unsteady. "Are you okay?"

Ty deliberately made light of the situation.
"Yeah, but the window doesn't look very
good."

Mary Ellen looked at the glassless window
and back to Ty. "What happened?"

"That's what we'd like to know," the factory
manager said.

Mary Ellen was confused when Ty broke into
German. The maneuver meant she couldn't
understand his explanation. It was intentional,

she knew that. The squeeze he gave her hand told her that he'd explain it all to her later.

Some of the factory manager's antagonism dissipated at Ty's knowledge of German and his willingness to answer questions.

Bertha barreled onto the scene a few minutes later and stirred things up again. "What is going on here? Mr. Stevenson, what have you done?"

Mary Ellen's hackles rose at Bertha's instant assumption that Ty had been responsible for the mess. She was about to confront the stout tour guide when Ty caught her eye and frowned warningly. Hard though it was, Mary Ellen held her tongue.

Ty didn't need anyone to come to his defense. He handled Bertha with an effective brand of sardonic humor. "Why, Bertha, how kind of you to come make sure I'm all right. You're so conscientious."

Bertha glared at a spot two inches above Ty's right shoulder before turning to question the factory manager. Her entire attitude switched from belligerent to apologetic as she dealt with him. Bertha, too, spoke in German. "I'm so sorry that this happened, Herr Müller. In all the years I've been a tour guide I've never had any trouble like this before."

The factory manager nodded.

Since she couldn't follow the conversation, Mary Ellen didn't know if that was a good sign or not.

"Apparently two men threw something at

this member of your tour group," Herr Müller told Bertha. "One of my men came in and found the two making their escape through the broken window. We have called the police, they should be arriving any moment."

Bertha was not pleased. "The police?"

"That's right." Herr Müller stood firm. "There has been a great deal of damage and we need to find those responsible."

Bertha turned to Ty and demanded, "Who started the fight?"

Ty corrected her in English. "It wasn't actually a fight. One of the men ran in here and started twirling something over his head, I'm not sure what it was. I ducked and the weapon, if you could call it that, hit the window and broke it."

Bertha wasn't satisfied. "What about all these broken clocks?"

"The guy's aim wasn't very good. After the window he hit the clocks."

"Did you get a good look at the men?" the manager wanted to know.

Ty nodded and his expression hardened. "I'd recognize them if I saw them again."

The police arrived and asked many of the same questions that Bertha and the factory manager had.

Bertha was having conniptions because of the delay. "This is ruining my schedule!" she could be heard to mutter again and again.

"Did you know the two men?" the police asked Ty.

"Not by name, no," he answered.

"Then how did you know them?"

"I'd seen them before."

"When?"

"When the tour was in Copenhagen."

"Do you think these two men may be following you?"

"It's possible."

"Why?"

Ty decided it would be wiser not to open that can of worms, so he shrugged and shook his head.

The police couldn't complain too much. Ty had been able to give them a detailed description of both men, which had been confirmed by the workman who'd been the first one to enter the room after the fracas. The police continued their questioning before being convinced that Ty knew no more. Finally they released him, and the rest of the tour group, allowing them to continue on their way.

When they were settled back on the bus, Mary Ellen wanted to hear Ty's explanation—all of it, not just the condensed version, and in English.

The only problem was that he wasn't talking. At first she blamed his silence on the aftermath of the police interrogation. After all, he had been put through intensive questioning, and that was enough to put anyone off.

But it didn't take Mary Ellen long to realize that there was more to it than that. Ty was withdrawing from her—not physically, perhaps, but emotionally. His monosyllabic responses to her concerned inquiries left her in no doubt that he wanted to be left alone. Even worse, she felt his isolation deepen with every mile they traveled.

Frustration and dread ate away at her heart. The first was caused by the inability to carry on a private discussion on the bus, the latter by the fear that he was planning to leave her.

Mary Ellen's fears were well founded. Ty was indeed making plans to leave. As he stared out the bus window he cursed himself for having underestimated Mr. Q's two goons. They had been able to find their way out of a paper bag, had in fact been clever enough to follow him. For how long? How long had he been putting Mary Ellen in jeopardy?

The plan that had seemed so expedient when he'd contemplated it in Monte Carlo now took on a new gravity. He'd never dreamt that the two incompetents would locate him on this bus tour, or that they would take such rash action as they had in the cuckoo clock factory. The discovery threw a new light on the seemingly unrelated things that had occurred earlier in the tour. No doubt being marooned above Innsbruck had been another result of their handiwork.

Fury darkened Ty's expression and colored his judgment. He should never have gotten Mary Ellen mixed up in this. She'd already been put in danger once as a result of his foolishness. What if Mary Ellen had been standing next to him when this latest attack came? What if she'd been hit instead of the window or the damn clocks? It could easily have happened. Too easily.

Awareness brought with it a sense of responsibility. If he left the tour, Mary Ellen would be safe and he'd have a better chance of finding the men who were following him. And when he did, he'd make sure that they'd regret ever having taken this assignment.

Ty remained caught up in his thoughts as the bus belatedly arrived in Paris. Even after they'd checked into their hotel and gone to their room, he remained quiet.

Mary Ellen had honored his desire for privacy as long as she could, but she couldn't stand the tension anymore. He was standing beside the window, staring out at the street below, when she took her courage in hand and forced the issue.

"You're getting ready to leave, aren't you." Her voice was flat, but her eyes were brimming with accusation.

He turned to face her. "Marielle . . ."

The way he said her name told her she was right. "I knew it."

"Listen to me. These guys' pranks have become a little too hazardous. The situation is no longer amusing. You could get hurt."

"So could you."

"I'll be fine. I always land on my feet, you know that."

Mary Ellen turned away and tried to get a

grip on her emotions. She knew he would be leaving her soon, she'd accepted that fact, but she couldn't accept his leaving while he was still in danger. "Ty, don't leave. Not yet."

"It's for your own good, Marielle."

Those were the same words he'd used seven years go when he'd left her then. *God protect me from things that are for my own good,* she thought to herself with bitterness.

"I don't want to put your safety in jeopardy," Ty said.

"The German police have a detailed description of the two men. They won't get very far before being caught." *Let him stay now,* she prayed, *and I'll give him up later without a fight.*

Someone must have been listening, because her prayer was answered. "All right, I'll stay," Ty murmured.

"Thank you." She wrapped her arms around him and hugged him.

Ty smoothed back her hair in a tender gesture. "Don't thank me yet. I'm staying because if the police don't catch the jerks, they'll come here looking for me, and I'd rather they found me than found you all alone."

Whatever his reasoning, Mary Ellen was just relieved that he wasn't leaving yet. The strength of her embrace communicated as much to Ty.

His teasing groan at the tightness of her hold alleviated the tense emotions of the moment.

"Sorry." Embarrassed, Mary Ellen released

him. "It's been a long day, I think I'll go take a shower and change."

Ty delayed her departure by catching her hand in his. "Don't change too much." He trailed his fingers down her flushed cheek. "I want you to stay just the way you are."

Her smile was wobbly. "Thanks, I needed that."

While Mary Ellen took her shower, Ty placed a phone call to Lars in Copenhagen. He needed more information, and Lars was the only one who could give it to him.

Lars was pleased to hear from him. "Ty! How's it going?"

"Not well. Those two goons our friend Mr. Q hired found me this morning at a cuckoo clock factory."

"Cuckoo clocks?"

"Yeah, those two fit right in. What have you found out about them?"

"Their names are Pierre and Josef. Pierre is described as being short with dark hair. Josef is tall, thin, with very little hair. They are both reputed to have very little in the brain department as well."

"They managed to find me," Ty retorted, "So they must have some brains."

"Maybe it was just luck."

"Whatever it was, I'm not happy about it. I had to answer questions from the police in Germany."

"The police?" Lars repeated.

After Ty finished his explanation, Lars told him, "I don't believe it."

"Dumb though they may be, they could easily have hurt someone." The wry humor left Ty's voice. "I don't like taking that risk."

"Ah, you worry about your girlfriend, hmmm?"

"That's one way of putting it." Ty could just imagine Mary Ellen's reaction at being called his "girlfriend."

"Not getting serious, are you, Ty?"

"Who, me?"

"Uh-oh." Lars was practically chortling with glee. "I was right. You always answer a question with a question when someone gets too close to the truth."

Ty was not amused. "Look, stop trying to psychoanalyze me and just keep on top of this situation with Mr. Q, Pierre, and . . . what's the other one's name?"

"Josef. And I am keeping on top of it, as you put it. Our contacts in Monte Carlo assure me that it should only be a matter of days before the really big guys catch up with Mr. Q."

"I hope they're right."

Lars became serious. "Ty, I feel so bad about this. I was the one who got you involved in the first place."

"Forget it. You've helped me out of a tight spot more than once. It was past time that I return the favor."

"Speaking of return, I've been asked to inquire when you might be returning to the racing circuit."

"I'm not sure."

"We're getting a little old for this life, hmm?" Lars suggested. He'd made no secret of the fact that he would be retiring after the next race.

"You may be right," Ty conceded. Out of the corner of his eye he noticed Mary Ellen coming out of the bathroom.

Seeing that Ty was on the phone she joined him on the bed where he was sitting. Ever so casually she shifted her position until she was directly behind him, so he couldn't see what she was doing. A very feminine grin crossed her face as she unwrapped the generous bath sheet from her otherwise bare body. Holding a fistful of the terry cloth material in each hand, she proceeded to slip her arms around him. Her action served to enclose Ty and herself in the misty warmth of the bath sheet.

"You still there?" Lars asked a distracted Ty.

"Uh, yeah."

Mary Ellen grinned at Ty's distracted reply and leaned closer, rubbing her bare breasts against his back.

The air left Ty's lungs with a whoosh and his heartbeat doubled.

"Was there anything else you wanted me to check on?" Lars asked Ty.

Mary Ellen stepped up her seductive attack by nibbling on the nape of Ty's neck.

"No. I'll be in touch." Ty didn't even give Lars time to say good-bye before he hung up.

"Come here, you!" Ty grabbed hold of Mary Ellen's arm and tugged her around until she was draped across his lap. The bath sheet was now twisted around her body in a way reminiscent of a *Playboy* layout, leaving more silky skin uncovered than covered. The wanton image was reinforced by the fact that she'd washed her hair but hadn't blown it dry.

"You look positively wicked," he noted. His eyes were much more expressive as they wandered over her with frank appreciation.

Mary Ellen was too intent on unbuttoning Ty's shirt to be concerned about her appearance.

"Your hair's still wet," he muttered in a husky voice. "You're going to catch cold."

"With you to keep me warm?" She peeled off his shirt and teased the warmth of his skin with the damp ends of her hair.

His moan warned her that his restraint was gone. "I'm going to do more than keep you warm, Marielle. I'm going to set you on fire and then I'm going to make you melt."

Ty was true to his word. He caressed every inch of her body, slowly and passionately. Excitement flared as he revisited those secret spots that gave her pleasure. He knew exactly where and how she liked to be touched, when to linger and when to rush. The sensitive skin behind her ears, the supple column of her throat, the creamy slopes of her breasts—all of her body's curves and inlets were treated to the most tantalizing loving imaginable. She was blinded by the white-hot ecstasy he evoked with his skillful fingers and wicked mouth.

He urged her to voice her fantasies and pleasures, and then set about fulfilling them. She flamed for him before he, too, succumbed to the fire burning between them. It seemed appropriate that such a wild sensual experience should have taken place in Paris, the City of Light, the City for Lovers.

The real city tour of Paris began early the next morning. They covered so much so fast that Mary Ellen's head was reeling. When she said as much to Ty, he claimed that the feeling was probably a result of last night's steamy session of lovemaking.

"You may be right," she agreed with a grin.

Everyone had their own favorite stop on the tour. Personally, Mary Ellen was looking forward to visiting the Cathedral of Notre Dame.

Ty was no newcomer to Paris, so while he enjoyed Mary Ellen's enthusiasm, he didn't get sidetracked by the sights. Instead he kept his eyes open for any sign of Pierre and Josef. His vigilance was rewarded when he spotted them loitering in the vicinity of Notre Dame. This time Ty intended to beat the two culprits at their own game.

While Mary Ellen may have been excited at the prospect of finally stepping inside Notre Dame after having read and heard so much about it, Archie did not share the feeling.

"Another church?" he groaned.

"This isn't just another church," Viola corrected him. "This is the cathedral where Quasimodo, the Hunchback of Notre Dame, hung out in Victor Hugo's novel."

"The Hunchback, huh?" Archie looked intrigued. "I dressed like him one year for Halloween."

"This is the first of the great churches to have flying buttresses," Mitzi inserted.

"Flying what?" Archie repeated. "Do they look like Quasimodo?"

"No. *Flying buttresses* describes an architectural style," Mitzi explained.

"Oh." With that Archie lost interest.

Mary Ellen did not allow Archie's apathy to diminish her own excitement. "Notre Dame! Mary, Queen of Scots was married here, Napoleon was crowned here, and I can't believe *I'm* really here!"

"Want me to pinch you?" Ty asked her while keeping one eye on Pierre and Josef. The two were unsuccessfully trying to blend into the background.

Mary Ellen refused Ty's teasing offer, unaware of his distraction.

"Worldwind tour group, over here!" Bertha gathered everyone around her before beginning her lecture on the history of Notre Dame. "The location of the cathedral has been a religious site since the time when a Roman-Gallic temple stood here."

"I'll bet Bertha was giving tours even then,"

Sheldon murmured in an undertone to Irma and Mary Ellen.

"Notice the intricate carving around the three front portals. As we walk inside, pay special attention to the glorious stained-glass rose window over the entrance," the tour guide commanded. "It is seven hundred years old."

For once everyone was eager to obey Bertha's order.

But there were even more impressive sights to be seen from the middle of the cathedral, where simply by turning her head Mary Ellen could see three rose windows. Sunlight poured through the chromatic glass, turning each huge rose-shaped window into a brilliant tapestry of light. Colored light. Wheels of fire.

"I think they're beautiful," Irma exclaimed.

"Me too," Mary Ellen turned to get Ty's opinion, only to find him missing.

"He was here a minute ago," she muttered to herself. Where had he gone? "Have you seen Ty?" she asked Sheldon and Irma.

"I thought I saw him go on up ahead with the rest of the group," Irma answered.

Mary Ellen heaved a sigh of relief. There was nothing to get upset about. She was simply overreacting because of yesterday's fiasco at the cuckoo clock factory.

Outside the cathedral Josef was looking at Pierre with disapproval. "You want to jump Stevenson in a church?"

"Don't tell me you're allergic to churches?" Pierre demanded in a sarcastic hiss.

"I do not approve of violence in the House of the Lord."

"Listen, Josef, God already knows what you've been doing for a living. This won't come as any surprise to Him."

Josef grimaced. "What is your plan?"

"Nothing fancy this time. I'm getting back to basics. That's where we got into trouble before. Trying to ambush Stevenson in the dungeon of that castle, marooning them on top of the mountain, tossing bolas at him in the cuckoo clock factory; those were all great plans but too elaborate. So my plan this time is very simple. We isolate Stevenson from the rest of the group and then we jump him." Pierre patted himself on the shoulder. "I know this cathedral like the back of my hand. There are plenty of places to get the job done."

Inside the cathedral Mary Ellen was still looking for Ty. She couldn't see him in the group crowded around Bertha. The cathedral itself was fairly crowded with other guided groups of tourists and individual sightseers. Perhaps Ty had decided to investigate the cathedral on his own. She knew he hated being led anywhere.

Hoping to find him Mary Ellen left the group. Her search led her into the more deserted area of the side aisles of the nave. Where before she had felt almost dwarfed by the cathedral's vast height, here she was suddenly aware of the dark shadows.

This may not have been a very smart thing to

do, going off by myself like this, she thought to herself with a tiny shiver.

A moment later she felt herself being grabbed. A hand placed over her mouth prevented her from screaming as she was dragged behind a column!

CHAPTER FOURTEEN

"It's me," Ty whispered in Mary Ellen's ear. "Don't make any noise. Do you understand?" He waited for her nod before removing his hand from her mouth. "Good."

Ty rewarded her with a brief kiss. His lips were warm and alive with hunger, but the caress was over before she had time to respond.

"Don't move." Ty breathed the words of caution against her parted lips.

Mary Ellen obeyed his command, stifling the shiver that threatened to slip down her spine.

With an imperceptible nod of his head Ty indicated the reason for their stealth.

There stood two men, one tall, one short. Both were obviously looking for someone.

"You were supposed to be keeping an eye on

Stevenson," the short one was complaining to the tall one. "How could you lose him?"

"It's not my fault," the tall one retorted. "You always blame everything on me."

"This is not the time to indulge in a fit of temperament."

"Then stop blaming everything on me! I followed Stevenson just like you said. You saw him leave the rest of the tour."

"That's right," the short one agreed. "I saw him go off on his own. *You* were supposed to go after him and jump him."

The short man came a few steps closer and then stamped his foot. "We've lost him! Let's not waste any more time in here. He must have gone outside. Come on, let's look."

Both men left.

Once the men were safely out of earshot, Mary Ellen whispered, "Those are the thugs who are after you?"

Ty nodded. "Stay here."

He left her to stealthily follow the men out of the cathedral.

Mary Ellen had no intention of staying behind, not knowing if Ty was all right. Besides, there were two bad guys against one. Surely she could help even the odds.

Outside the cathedral Pierre and Josef were getting leery.

"I don't like this," Pierre said. "I don't see Stevenson out here either. He may be setting a trap for us."

The possibility didn't surprise Josef. "I told

you it would be bad luck to try and take care of business in a church."

Pierre glared at Josef. "Be quiet and grab that cab."

Ty came out of Notre Dame in time to see Pierre and Josef hurrying into a cab. He raced after them and hailed the next cab.

Determined not to be left behind, Mary Ellen had followed Ty out of the cathedral. She scooted into the back of his cab right after him. "I'm coming with you," she stated in no uncertain terms.

Ty's expression was both disapproving and exasperated. "I don't have time to argue with you now." In the same breath he ordered the cabdriver in French to follow the cab ahead of them.

The Parisian cabby grinned and floored the gas pedal. The cab took off like a rocket, its abrupt acceleration flinging Mary Ellen sideways into Ty's arms.

"Of all the times to throw yourself at me!" he murmured with a devilish smile.

Mary Ellen kept her eyes open for as long as she could. She recognized the Louvre as they flew past it, almost hitting three other cars as their driver attempted to keep up with the other cab.

The trip around the Place de la Concorde was a real nightmare. Their driver cut in front of other cars, ignored stop signs, yield signs, all signs, in his reckless haste to keep the other cab in sight.

Mary Ellen withstood it by placing both hands over her eyes and occasionally peeking through her fingers, only to gasp and close her eyes again.

Ty was in his element. He recognized their driver's abilities and praised him, promising him another four hundred francs if they kept up with the other cab.

Meanwhile Josef was peering out of the back window of their cab. "We're being followed!"

"I know that, idiot!" Pierre's face was florid. The day was not going at all as he had planned. "Why do you think our driver is going so fast?"

"You think it is Stevenson who is following us?"

"I can't imagine who else it could be. Lose them!" Pierre curtly ordered their driver.

"They know we're following them," Ty noted from his watchful position in the back-seat. Since he was speaking in French, Mary Ellen had no idea what he was saying. "Keep up with them," he instructed their driver.

Mary Ellen gave a muffled shriek as their driver pulled the cab into the oncoming lane of traffic to overcome a slow bus ahead of them. They passed the bus and avoided a head-on collision by what looked to her to be mere centimeters. Other drivers honked their horns and shouted obscenities out of their rolled-down windows. Several clenched fists and rude gestures were also apparent as their driver stayed hot on the trail.

Down the tree-lined Champs Elysées they

went, past the Arc de Triomphe. A dozen broad avenues fanned out from the famous monument and fed swirling traffic around it. For a while there Mary Ellen was certain they were going to drive right through the monument, if they didn't ram into it first!

Pierre and Josef's driver continued to employ defensive maneuvers in an attempt to lose Ty. At a curt command from Pierre the driver abruptly cut across three lanes of traffic and took a turn off.

Ty's cabby followed suit. Cars screeched to a halt, but they made it—just. Mary Ellen was fatalistically expecting to hear the sound of a siren behind them; the police if they were lucky, an ambulance if they weren't.

The wild chase came to a head a few minutes later. Pierre and Josef's cab sped up and whizzed through an intersection without stopping, which caused the two cars that had the right of way to swerve in order to avoid an accident. The cars didn't hit the cab, but they sideswiped each other.

In a classic replay from a slapstick comedy the cars skidded and hit a heavily loaded vegetable cart. Fresh produce flew in every direction, raining down on passersby.

The drivers of the two cars were unharmed, by the accident at least. They'd jumped out of their dented cars and were threatening each other with clenched fists. A crowd gathered within seconds, urging them on.

Ty's cabby slammed on the brakes. The intersection was effectively blocked. There was no way they could continue following the other cab now.

"Damn!" Ty sighed and shook his head.

The cabby shrugged philosophically. He and Ty exchanged several manly slaps on the back and a stream of French.

"Come on." Ty turned to Mary Ellen, whose head was still spinning from the car chase.

"Where are we going?"

"To get another cab. Just to be on the safe side."

Being on the safe side sounded very good to Mary Ellen.

"What time is it?" she asked as Ty took her across the street and away from the bedlam in the intersection.

"Noon. Why?"

"I promised Hank that we'd meet him, Viola, and Archie for lunch. Archie has a surprise."

"I don't know if I can take any more surprises today," Ty murmured as he hailed a cab on the next street corner.

"If we don't show up they'll worry about us."

"All right. Where are we supposed to meet them?"

Mary Ellen took a sheet of paper from her purse and read the name and address of the café.

"We're not too far from there now," Ty noted. "We'll just have the cab drop us off."

"You think it will be safe?"

"Yes. Pierre and Josef have no way of trailing

us now. They're too busy trying to make their own getaway at the moment." Ty was sure that it wouldn't be long before the two were following him again. No doubt they'd be waiting at the hotel, so it was just as well that he and Mary Ellen stay out for a while.

Hank, Viola, and Archie were already seated at a table waiting for them.

"Sorry we're late," Mary Ellen apologized.

"We were delayed in traffic around the Place de la Concorde," Ty inserted with a grin in Mary Ellen's direction. "It was fierce."

"Hey, isn't that where the guillotine was set up?" Archie asked Ty. "Mitzi told me that the king of France, one of those Louis guys, got his head chopped off there. So did the queen."

"Archie, please," Mary Ellen protested. "Not when we're about to eat." The violent legacy of the Place de la Concorde only confirmed what she'd thought as they'd been barreling around it—the place could be dangerous to one's health.

"After you two disappeared from Notre Dame, I was afraid you weren't going to be able to make it for lunch," Viola confessed. "Bertha was fit to be tied when she discovered you were gone and that she was two people short. You know how she is about keeping a proper head count."

"Something came up," Ty replied.

A bored waiter appeared a moment later to take their order. Everyone was surprised to hear Archie speaking to the waiter in slow but accurate French. Archie beamed at the open-mouthed response he got from his father.

"Where'd you learn to speak French?" Hank asked his son. "I thought you were taking Spanish in school."

"We are." Archie tapped his trusty Walkman. "I've been listening to French language tapes since we left home."

"I'm impressed!" Viola said.

"So am I," Mary Ellen seconded.

Unfortunately their waiter was not impressed. When Archie spoke again, he answered in a rapid Parisian stream that the boy couldn't hope to follow.

Archie painstakingly explained that he couldn't understand and asked the waiter to speak more slowly.

Archie may not have understood the rude reply the waiter made, but Ty did and he retaliated by matching the waiter's knowledge of French insults. Startled, the waiter decided to heed Ty's curt warning about the consequences of any further discourtesy.

"Is something wrong?" Mary Ellen asked Ty.

Ty shook his head. "Just a little misunderstanding. It's all cleared up now. Go ahead, Archie, finish ordering for us."

The thirteen-year-old did, hesitatingly at first but then with increasing confidence as the waiter spoke slowly and understandably.

"I'm impressed," Ty stated.

"Me too," Mary Ellen said. In an undertone

she added to Ty, "With you. That was a very nice thing to do."

"What was?"

"Having that little talk with the waiter. He was being rude, wasn't he?"

"He was being uncooperative," Ty agreed.

Archie interrupted their low-voiced conversation to ask Ty, "Where did you learn French?"

"I've spent some time in Monte Carlo," Ty replied.

The others looked intrigued, but the news came as no surprise to Mary Ellen. Ty had mentioned before that he'd met Mr. Q in Monte Carlo. Since both gambling and race-car driving were very popular there, Ty no doubt spent a great deal of time kicking up his heels in the famous playground of the rich. Jet setters. The fast life. A life she had no part in. His life.

"I've always wanted to go to Monte Carlo," Viola said. "Is it as beautiful as they say?"

"Yes." Ty wondered why Mary Ellen was frowning.

Mary Ellen wondered why Ty was looking at her so closely. She hadn't given herself away, had she? No, he couldn't possibly know that she'd been brooding over their differences. Not that brooding did any good. At least she could enjoy the here and now.

The waiter arrived with their food, and conversation lagged as everyone dug in. They'd each ordered something different from the

242

menu. Ty had selected the shrimp provençale. On Ty's recommendation Mary Ellen had chosen the grilled fish. Hank went with the veal, Viola the roast chicken. Archie made a point of staying away from the goose liver and the breast of pigeon. He settled for French onion soup and a side order of *pommes frites*, french fries.

They all agreed on fresh fruit sorbet for dessert.

In keeping with their European surroundings the group lingered over their meal. Conversation inevitably ran toward the upcoming end of the tour.

"These past two weeks have gone by quickly," Viola said. "Tomorrow we leave Paris for Brussels, and then it's back to London." As if realizing how down she was sounding Viola hastily added, "We have seen a lot, though."

"And been through a lot together," Ty murmured, his gaze intent on Mary Ellen's face.

"That's true," she agreed. Even so, she knew that what she and Ty had been through and shared would not make any difference to the eventual outcome of this trip. He would still go his way, and she hers.

"Hank and I thought we'd take Archie out to Versailles this afternoon," Viola interjected, unaware of Mary Ellen's melancholy. "It was a difficult choice. There's so much to see and so little time."

Mary Ellen's eyes clouded. She was very much aware of how little time was left. But she didn't want to waste any of it feeling sorry for herself. So when Viola began discussing other tour members' plans for the day, Mary Ellen gratefully picked up on her comments. Anything to stop her from thinking about Ty's inevitable departure. "Sheldon and Irma said they planned on going to the top of the Eiffel Tower this afternoon. The view of Paris is supposed to be wonderful from there."

"What are your plans for the rest of the day?" Viola asked Mary Ellen.

"I'm not sure. Ty, what do you think—" Mary Ellen never completed her sentence, because Ty jumped out of his seat in the middle of it and grabbed the newspaper being read by the man at the next table.

The other restaurant patron was not pleased at having his paper torn from his hands while he was reading it and he put up a fight.

Seeing that the man had no intention of giving up his paper even for a second, Ty was forced to offer him money for it. "I'll give you forty francs for this paper." Forty francs was roughly the equivalent of five American dollars, but getting the paper was worth it to Ty.

The offer was accepted and the paper eagerly handed over. Sensing the makings of a huge profit the man indicated several girlie magazines he had sitting on the table. "I've got some magazines here too. Do you want to buy them too? I'll give you a good price."

"No, thanks, just the paper will be fine."

Confused by Ty's strange behavior Hank, Viola, and Archie all looked to Mary Ellen for an explanation.

Embarrassed by all the attention she lamely explained, "Ty goes crazy if he doesn't read his paper every day."

"So I see," Viola murmured with a shake of her head.

Ty returned to their table with a smile on his face and the French newspaper in his hands.

"Are you happy now?" Mary Ellen asked him through gritted teeth. She hated being the center of attention or the cause of a scene.

Ty didn't mind the limelight in the least. "Yes. Very happy."

Mary Ellen gave him a look of exasperation. "I'm glad."

So was Ty. Glad that it was all over. For the newspaper he'd just obtained for such an inflated price contained one very important article. A small-time gambler, known as Mr. Q, had been found dead in his hotel room in Monte Carlo. The police said that the cause of his death was as yet unknown.

All Ty knew was that the game of in pursuit was finally over. Now all he had to do was discuss the terms of surrender with Pierre and Josef.

CHAPTER FIFTEEN

"It was a good thing that minor car accident prevented Stevenson's cab from following us," Josef murmured from behind the newspaper he was supposed to be reading. "What makes you think Stevenson will be returning to the hotel?"

"He has to sleep sometime," Pierre replied from behind another newspaper. "And when he does, we'll catch him."

"But we've been sitting here for two hours now," Josef grouched. "I don't like it. I've got a funny feeling about this."

"You've had a funny feeling since we began this job."

"And I've been right. We should never have taken this job." Josef's expression became forlorn. "Nothing has gone right. Not one single thing."

"Stop complaining," Pierre ordered impatiently. "So we've had a bit of bad luck. That only means that things will be going our way now."

"If that's true, then what's taking Stevenson so long to get back?"

"It's only early afternoon," Pierre retorted. "Give it more time. Stevenson may be a bit young to require an afternoon nap, but I believe he plans on sharing a little afternoon delight with his lady friend. And for that I'm sure they will return to their hotel room."

"Maybe Stevenson is staying away because he figures we're here waiting for him. And he could have sex in any vacant hotel room in Paris, he doesn't have to come back here," Josef pointed out.

Pierre bent down a corner of the paper and glared at him. "You have no poetry," he declared with dramatic gusto.

Josef was bewildered. "What does poetry have to do with anything?"

"Never mind. I told you that I checked with the desk and made sure that Stevenson has not checked out. Why should he pay for another room when he can return here for free?"

"Because *we* are here waiting for him."

"He doesn't know that."

"How can you be sure?"

Pierre's newspaper rustled and his voice lowered to a hushed whisper of excitement. "I can be sure because Stevenson just walked into the lobby. I told you he would return!"

Ty had no difficulty in finding Pierre and Josef. They were the only two men in the lobby reading their newspapers upside down.

"You go on up to our room," Ty told Mary Ellen. "I'll join you in a few minutes."

"Where are you going?"

"For a walk."

"Do you think that's safe?"

"Trust me."

Something about the confidence of his voice made her believe that Ty knew what he was doing. "Be careful," she murmured.

"Always." He smiled and gave her a lingering kiss. "I won't be too long."

That's what you think, Pierre thought to himself with a grin. Finally, success was so close that he could almost taste it! He watched Stevenson leave the lobby and then jabbed Josef with his elbow. "Come on, let's go get him!"

They tracked Ty as he walked down the street. Pierre could hardly believe his luck when he realized that Ty was walking away from, rather than toward, the main boulevards. If Ty continued at this rate they would soon reach an area of Paris that Pierre knew to be rough. No one would take any notice if a man happened to be mugged.

They turned a corner only to find that Ty had disappeared.

"We've lost him again," Josef practically wailed.

"Quiet. There he is." Pierre pointed ahead to where Ty was just leaving a store. He was now carrying a parcel in his hands.

Josef eyed the cord-wrapped parcel with curiosity. "What do you think he bought? Food?"

"What does it matter?"

"We've been so busy following Stevenson that we haven't had a chance to eat yet today," Josef pointed out to the accompaniment of a growl from his hungry stomach.

"Food can wait," Pierre declared. "Hurry up, he's walking faster. We have to keep up."

Their pace quickened to a near trot. Even so, they turned the next corner too late to see which direction Ty had taken. The street split into two; one fork went to the left and one to the right.

"You go that way," Pierre instructed Josef. "I'll look for him this way. This neighborhood is pretty deserted, we shouldn't have any problem finding him. Shout if you get him."

Pierre didn't have the chance to shout. As he was walking along the sidewalk, Ty appeared out of a deserted doorway and grabbed him.

"Pierre, I believe?" Ty drawled as he shoved the smaller man against the wall, hoisted him by his collar, and held him dangling so that Pierre's toes barely remained on the ground.

"Let me go!" Pierre croaked.

"No way."

"You are insane!"

"No, but I am damn angry," Ty replied in such a pleasant voice that Pierre panicked.

"My friend will be here in a moment and then you'll be sorry," Pierre threatened.

"I'm not the one who's going to be sorry. You and your pal Josef are." As he was speaking, Ty efficiently wrapped a length of thick cord around Pierre's wrists and tied it to the doorknob of the deserted building behind them. "There—that should keep you here for a while." Ty unwrapped the paisley scarf from around Pierre's neck and stuffed it into his mouth, thereby stifling his shout of protest.

"Now we'll just stay here until Josef comes back looking for you."

Knowing Josef's past track record Pierre was afraid that the wait might be long; but it wasn't.

Ty employed the same tactics with Josef as he had with Pierre. Strangely enough the taller man didn't put up much of a fight at all.

"I knew it would end like this," Josef stated with fatalistic resignation. "No good comes out of doing business in a church. I told Pierre. I told him we should forget this job."

"You really should have taken his advice," Ty told a furious Pierre. "Especially now that your employer is deceased."

Pierre's eyes bulged open with surprise.

"Aha, you didn't know that did you? I didn't think so. Maybe if you'd bothered reading the paper instead of hiding behind it, we might have been able to settle this more easily," Ty murmured.

"What are you going to do with us?" Josef

asked. Since he showed no signs of fighting, Ty hadn't gagged him.

"The way I see it there are three choices. I can turn you over to the authorities, or I can turn you over to the mob that probably did in your former employer. I'm sure they'd be very interested in tidying up any loose ends, and I fear you two gentlemen just might be a pair of loose ends."

Josef hurriedly pleaded their case. "Mr. Stevenson, we got in over our heads—a human mistake, surely. We meant you no harm, and now that our former employer is gone, you need have no fear of ever seeing us again. The job we were hired to do is over, forgotten."

"Over," Ty agreed. "But not forgotten. You see, gentlemen, I might have been a little more forgiving had your silly pranks only involved me. But you endangered a woman whom I care very much for, and I find that hard to forgive or forget."

"I did not want to leave her up on the mountain," Josef maintained. "That was the only time we involved her. We tried to be very careful."

"Not careful enough." Ty's voice was dark and menacing.

Josef swallowed nervously. "What are you going to do?"

"I should turn you over to the authorities, but that would mean having to answer a lot of questions, and there's always the chance that you'll make bail and skip the country. Option number two would probably mean your going the way Mr. Q went. There is, however, option number three."

"Which is?"

"That you agree to restitution. Repaying your debt to society, as it were. You see, it's this way, guys. If it were up to me I'd just as soon see you rot in prison or end up at the bottom of the Seine. But my girlfriend doesn't approve of violence. She always tries to see the good in people. Since she's been the innocent one in this mess, I think it only fair that you repay her."

"How? We have no money left, we spent it all on following you," Josef told Ty.

"You'll repay her by volunteering to work for a group called Hunger Prevention. They have an office here in Paris. Since you will be doing this out of the goodness of your hearts, of course there will be no payment. You will work for Hunger Prevention, full time, six days a week, for free, for the period of a year. And to make sure that you keep to your end of the bargain, I'll have a few of my friends here in Paris keeping track of you. So don't get any notions about skipping out on your responsibilities. If you do, I'll have the mob on you so fast your head will spin."

Ty gave them both a moment to consider their options before asking, "Well, what's it to be?"

"I agree," Josef said.

"And you?" Ty removed Pierre's gag so that he could answer.

"You're crazy!" Pierre exclaimed hoarsely.

"Does that mean you want me to go to the police?"

"No."

"I see." Ty shrugged. "Okay, it's your choice. I'll let the mob know you were in cahoots with Mr. Q."

"No!"

"You're running out of options," Ty warned Pierre.

"All right, all right. I agree. But it is highway robbery." A weasel to the end Pierre tried to bargain. "Six months without pay is much more reasonable than a year."

"Listen, buddy, after what you've done you're lucky to even be walking." Ty's voice resumed its menacing tone. "I wouldn't push it, if I were you."

Pierre hurriedly backed off. "All right. I accept."

"Good. Now, you will report for duty first thing tomorrow morning. The people at Hunger Prevention know nothing of our agreement, and the situation is to remain that way. As far as they are concerned, you two are just a pair of do-gooders who want to lend a helping hand to the needy in this world. And remember, it you make one false move or try to shirk your responsibilities, you won't be in this world for long. Is that understood?"

Pierre and Josef both nodded.

"Good. Ah, here comes my friend Henri. Think of him as your parole officer. You are to report to him once a week, and he will be keeping close tabs on you. He will stay with you and escort you to the Hunger Prevention office in the morning. Now, don't look so disheartened," Ty said as he untied them. "Remember, gentlemen, penance is good for the soul."

Ty's soul was much lighter as he left Pierre and Josef in Henri's more than capable hands. As the bouncer in a Parisian private club Henri knew how to handle problems.

Now he could return to the hotel and direct all of his attention to Mary Ellen.

She was waiting for him when he entered their room. He was beginning to recognize that look, as if she were trying to decide whether to hug him or hit him.

He made the choice for her by taking her in his arms. "Stop worrying. It's all over."

"Oh, no." She placed her hands on his chest, her fingers resting on the soft leather of his jacket. "You're not getting off the hook that easily! Tell me everything," she demanded. "And in English. You can start with your strange behavior at the restaurant. What was in that newspaper?"

Ty attempted to sidestep the issue. "Look, I told you that the chase is over. Pierre and Josef won't be bothering either of us again."

"That sounds ominous. What did you do to them? And how do you know that Mr. Q won't hire someone else instead?"

"Mr. Q won't be hiring anyone, because he died rather suddenly. That's why I grabbed the newspaper. I saw the brief notice about it."

Although she wouldn't wish death on anyone, Mary Ellen was relieved to hear that the man who had wanted to punish Ty was no longer a threat. "What about Pierre and Josef?"

"We talked things over and settled everything amicably," Ty replied with breezy vagueness. "They agreed that there was no point in continuing the matter."

"That's it, then? It's really over?"

"Yes. And I thought we'd celebrate."

"Really?" She ran her fingers along the slightly raspy line of his jaw. "That sounds interesting."

"You'll find it enjoyable, I'm sure."

She teasingly socked his arm. "You're so modest."

Ty released her and handed Mary Ellen her purse. "Come on, let's go."

"Now where are we going?"

"There's still some of the afternoon left and we're going to enjoy it. I'm going to give you a lovers' tour of Paris."

Mary Ellen resolutely quelled the realization that Ty no longer had any need to stay hidden on her bus tour. The danger was over. She knew what she had to do. But not yet. She blanked out the worries and fears, the dread and apprehension, even the suspicion that this was not the first lovers' tour Ty had given a woman in Paris.

The latter became harder to suppress when he took her to an exclusive women's boutique. The interior reminded Mary Ellen of a gilded birdcage, although few cages possessed expensive Louis XV chairs to perch on, nor did they have mauve carpeting.

The woman who approached them had a birdlike demeanor; her hand movements were quick and fluttery, her eyes dark and beady. She sized up the total cost of Mary Ellen's clothing in two seconds and dismissed her. Ty warranted closer examination, however.

"Ah! Monsieur Stevenson! Naughty boy!" The woman smiled and kissed Ty on both cheeks.

Mary Ellen was getting tired of having everyone break into French, or some other foreign language, just when things were getting interesting. She didn't like not being able to follow the conversation. She also didn't like the obvious fact that the woman knew Ty, which meant that he'd probably frequented this establishment before.

Ty broke off his conversation with the woman and brought Mary Ellen forward. "Madame St. Cloud, allow me to introduce Mary Ellen."

"Bonjour." Mary Ellen was rather proud of the way she said the French greeting. The move backfired on her when Madame St. Cloud replied in French.

Ty intervened. "Mary Ellen doesn't speak French."

"Oh." Madame St. Cloud looked at Mary Ellen as if she were some sort of cultural freak.

"You come here often?" Mary Ellen asked Ty.

"I drop by whenever I'm in Paris. Madame is a faithful follower of the racing circuit. Her late husband was Guy St. Cloud, one of the world's best drivers."

Privately Mary Ellen thought that the other woman was displaying an unseemly interest in Ty, but she kept her thoughts to herself. She knew nothing of Ty's life as a racer. She'd deliberately refrained from asking him about his career, his plans for the future, and Ty hadn't offered any information.

"What can I do for you, naughty boy?" Madame St. Cloud purred with the sexy inflection only a Frenchwoman possesses.

"I want to buy one of your creations for Mary Ellen."

Madame St. Cloud raised a penciled eyebrow and looked at Mary Ellen with new eyes.

A moment later Mary Ellen was being measured by Madame St. Cloud, who clucked as she worked with her tape measure.

"I have just the thing!" she declared a few moments later.

Mary Ellen waited until she'd left the room before turning to Ty and voicing her protest. "There's no need to buy me anything."

"Indulge me," he whispered in that sexy

drawl that warmed her heart and raised her blood pressure.

Madame St. Cloud returned with her creation.

Mary Ellen stared at the very naughty night-gown with equal parts of astonishment and disbelief.

"For my naughty eyes only," Ty murmured with a grin. "Try it on and see if it fits."

Mary Ellen actually blushed. "I may just have enough nerve to wear this for you," she muttered for his ears only, "but there's no way I'm going to put it on in public."

"I wasn't suggesting that you parade around the streets in it, just try it on in the fitting room."

"You just want to sneak a peek," she accused him. "It will fit, take my word for it." She looked at the bits of lace and satin. "There isn't enough there not to fit."

"Of course it will fit," Madame St. Cloud exclaimed. "I measured her myself. You will be pleased, naughty boy! Wait and see."

"It looks like I'll have to," Ty returned. "Wrap it up, we'll take it."

Ty silenced Mary Ellen's objections with a kiss.

As his tour progressed he bought her more— a bag of sinful chocolate-covered truffles, a gaudy souvenir of the Eiffel Tower, and a bouquet of fresh flowers from a flower vendor beside the Seine.

Mary Ellen linked her fingers through Ty's as

they strolled along the quai. "Notre Dame looks even more impressive from here, doesn't it?" she murmured.

Ty nodded.

"It's hard to believe that we were in there earlier this morning, when you were being chased by Pierre and Josef."

"Forget about it. Enjoy the view."

She enjoyed not only the view but also the company. Looking at the way the late-afternoon sun was hitting the stone of the cathedral and turning it pink, she was reminded that her time with Ty was almost over. From where they stood Notre Dame appeared to be constructed more of air than stone, the lightness and grace of its design very apparent from this angle. Yet for all its appearance of fragility the cathedral had survived the perils of time. Just as she would survive without Ty. Or would she?

"Hey, I recognize that frown," Ty said in a teasing voice. "It means you're getting hungry. And I know a place that has the most beautiful view of Paris, especially at twilight."

An inner voice warned her that time was slipping away and told her to enjoy while she could. "Where is this place?"

"Right up ahead. A dinner cruise along the Seine."

Dinner cruise conjured up the image of fancy clothing. "But I'm not dressed for it," Mary Ellen said.

"Sure you are. Come on."

Paris did look magical by twilight, especially

when seen from the river. The lights illuminating Notre Dame went on just as they began the cruise. As twilight fell, all of the city's monuments and bridges were lit with floodlights, giving them a special glow. Mary Ellen could see how Paris had gotten its nickname of the City of Light.

There was dancing after dinner to romantic music on a small, intimate dance floor. The combination made for tempting embraces. Mary Ellen's hand slid around his neck as she nestled her head against his shoulder. Ty responded by tugging her closer, so that she was resting even more snugly against him.

Dancing had now become merely an excuse to be in each other's arms. Ty's feet may have been barely moving in time to the music, but his hands were definitely on the move. They stroked up and down her spine in a soothing massage. Mary Ellen closed her eyes and enjoyed the feel of his lips seeking out her nape.

"I want to get you alone, away from all these people," Ty whispered in her ear, adding a tantalizing nibble to her earlobe.

"Me too," she concurred unsteadily.

Thankfully the cruise ended soon afterward. The trip back to the hotel was hazy for Mary Ellen, who was being seduced in the backseat of the cab by her passionate lover. When they arrived at the hotel, their driver had to clear his throat several times in order to get their attention.

There were more kisses in the tiny elevator.

Ty continued his seduction by whisking her in his arms the moment they were in their room. Mary Ellen returned the embrace with such abandon that they both stumbled, and bumped into something in the still-darkened room.

Ty reluctantly released her and turned on the lights. "I guessed as much. We just almost knocked over the vintage bottle of Champagne that I had sent up while we were out."

"I don't need Champagne," Mary Ellen whispered. "I already feel intoxicated."

Her admission made Ty forget all about opening the foil-wrapped bottle. Instead he opened the buttons of her blouse and peeled it and her jacket from her body.

While he continued undressing her, Mary Ellen was gladly returning the favor. Regardless of how many times she'd seen him nude, she continued to be amazed by him. She loved everything about him. The roguish light in his eyes, the scar beneath his jaw that he'd gotten as a child, the curve of his upper lip compared to the sensual fullness of his lower lip. And then there was his body; lean by some people's standards, but perfect by hers.

The hunger that had been building up on the boat's tiny dance floor, in the backseat of the cab, and in the cramped confines of the hotel elevator flared out of control. Ty kisses were ravenous, his caresses scandalous. She was thrilled by both and she desired more.

Her impatience matched his and things escalated quickly. Within seconds they were lying on the bed, neither one sure how they'd gotten there and neither one caring. Their union was fierce and all-consuming. Satisfaction came with stunning rapidity.

Later that night they finally did open the bottle of Champagne, sharing it and a bubble bath in an old-fashioned cast-iron tub that was big enough for both of them. They each sat at opposite ends of the tub. Mary Ellen's legs lay beside Ty's.

Ty held up his tulip-shaped, Champagne-filled glass and proposed a toast. "To the magic of Paris and you."

He touched his glass to hers. The crystal clinked with bell-like clarity.

"Now it's my turn," she murmured after they'd both taken a sip. "To the past two weeks and all the magic we've shared."

Ty was too taken in by the beauty of her smile to notice that she only referred to the past and not the future.

Leaning back Ty propped his elbows on the tub's rim and made himself comfortable. "Confess, aren't you glad that I suggested sharing this bathtub?"

"It was a brilliant idea." She shifted her foot so that it rubbed against his hip. "But do you realize that I still haven't modeled that naughty negligée you bought for me?"

Ty reached under the water to wrap his fingers around her ankle. "Don't start something that you can't finish," he warned her in a teasing growl.

"Me?" She fluttered her eyes with pretended innocence. "I was just—"

"I know exactly what you were doing." He lifted her foot and kissed the bubbles clinging to her instep. "Tantalizing me and generally driving me crazy with desire." His tongue curled to sneak between her dripping toes, seeking out the bubbles hiding there.

His teasing gesture had an arousing affect on her, an affect that was clearly visible through the bursting bubbles shielding her breasts.

Seeing her response Ty transformed his hold on her ankle to a hand-over-hand grip that moved up her calf to her knee as he reeled her in like a master fisherman until she was sitting on his lap. He positioned her so that he had one of her shapely legs on each side of him. They were now intimately close.

Her bent knees rose above the waterline to squeeze the sides of his torso as Ty bent his head and used his curling tongue on the slope of her breast. His arms encircled her, his hands resting on the small of her back to press her even closer. The water lapped around them as he rose against her, letting her feel the strength of his need—tempting but not fulfilling.

Mary Ellen experienced such a jolt of desire that she moaned his name. She leaned away, frightened by her utter breathlessness.

Her unspoken astonishment at his actions told him that she'd never made love in a bathtub before. Ty knew he had to acquaint her with the pleasures to be had.

"We can't . . . not here. . . ."

"How about here?" he suggested, moving his mouth on her skin.

"We'll drown. . . . Oh . . . Ty . . . ummm-mmm."

Ty kissed her closed eyes while his fingers slid from her breasts down to her navel and the smoothness of her abdomen. From there his gliding caresses sought and found her inner warmth.

"Yes . . . yes. . . . !" She returned his kisses with feverish intensity.

She was tingling all over, inside and out. Her needs were so high pitched already that she had to have more than his erotic finger-play. She needed all of him, right then and there.

"Now." She reached for him. Her bold fingers curled around him with an urgency that took his breath away.

He filled her guiding hand and soon filled her. She accepted all of him, enfolding him deep within her. She loved him as if there would be no tomorrow, as if this would be their last time together.

Ty remembered that sensual fervor the next morning, as they shared breakfast in their room instead of joining the rest of the group downstairs in the main dining room. When Mary Ellen informed him that it was time he return to Monte Carlo, he didn't take her seriously.

"There's no hurry," he said, certain that she must be kidding him.

"What's the point in waiting?" she countered in a calm voice as she buttered a croissant. The mere thought of food made her feel like choking, but the action kept her hands busy and disguised their trembling.

She'd gone over her options while Ty had slept. She'd known this moment was coming. She'd made a vow and she'd keep it. She'd promised herself to give him up without a fight, as long as he stayed with her until he was out of danger. He had. So she intended on ending it now, while she still had the strength to do so. Selfish though it sounded, she had to reject him before he rejected her yet again. It was the only way she'd be able to handle it.

"I took the liberty of packing your things," she told him. "It's been fun, but it's time to return to reality. I'm sure you're in a hurry to get back into the swing of your normal life now that the danger is over. Just as I am."

Ty abruptly realized that she really was serious. "What is this?" His frown reflected his displeasure and confusion. *She* was telling *him* good-bye?

"I would have thought it was obvious."

"Not to me it isn't." His voice was rough with anger at the way she was trying to give him the bum's rush. "Just two days ago you were begging me to stay and now suddenly you can't wait for me to leave? I don't get it."

"What's there to get?" she countered coolly. "We both knew it would end."

"Did we?"

"Yes. There were no promises given."

That was true, but he'd always assumed . . . Hell, what had he assumed? That she loved him as much as he loved her? If that were true, then how could she so calmly throw away what they had together?

Ty was dazed. He felt as if he'd been dealt a knockdown blow that he hadn't even seen coming. His eyes narrowed broodingly as he stared at her, trying to read her thoughts. But her expression was enigmatic. "Why are you doing this?"

"Come on, Ty, what's the big deal?" Mary Ellen even managed a scoffing smile. "I wanted a romantic fling while I was here in Europe, and you provided me with one. It was fun, but now it's over."

"Are you serious?" he demanded harshly. His jaw was clenched with anger. "This is really the way you want it?"

"Yes." Knowing she'd crumble at the least sign of his persuasive ways, she added a final throwaway comment she knew would madden him. "We can still be friends."

"Yeah, sure." Ty tossed down his napkin, grabbed his suitcase, and left without saying another word.

CHAPTER SIXTEEN

It hurt more than Mary Ellen would have thought possible. Her determination to go into this with her eyes open hadn't helped at all. The sound of Ty closing the door still hit her like a physical blow.

Gone. For the last time. Really gone.

Mary Ellen cried, even though she knew there wasn't time for that now. Bertha would be pounding on her door any minute demanding to know why she was late. Everyone else was probably already on the bus, waiting. So she wiped away the tears as soon as they fell and gathered up her belongings. She couldn't fall apart, not yet.

Her shaky control was sorely tested when Bertha saw that Ty was not accompanying

Mary Ellen downstairs. "Mr. Stevenson is going to make us late," the tour guide stated with disapproval.

"Mr. Stevenson had to leave," Mary Ellen explained in a strained voice.

"Leave?" Bertha was upset. "How can he leave? We are going on to Brussels in exactly five minutes!"

"Mr. Stevenson had to leave the tour here in Paris. Something came up."

"This is most unsatisfactory." Bertha glared at Mary Ellen's forehead. "We at Worldwind Tours seriously disapprove of people leaving helter-skelter."

Mary Ellen couldn't help it. The tears escaped her control again and flowed down her cheeks.

Bertha looked dismayed. "There, there." She awkwardly patted Mary Ellen on the shoulder. "It is nothing to cry about. If Mr. Stevenson had to leave, he had to leave." She shrugged philosophically. "We will carry on without him and have a good time, you will see. Here, now . . ." Bertha handed Mary Ellen a handkerchief. "Dry your tears. It will be all right. I'm not angry anymore."

Had Mary Ellen been thinking more clearly, she might have been surprised by Bertha's sudden maternal concern. As it was, she accepted the handkerchief with a great deal of embarrassment. "I'm sorry," she whispered unsteadily.

"Never mind."

Irma and Sheldon walked onto the scene at that point and drew their own conclusions when they saw the evidence of Mary Ellen's recent tears.

"What's going on here?" Irma demanded, jumping to Mary Ellen's defense like a tigress defending its young. She came to Mary Ellen and wrapped a comforting arm around her shoulder. Then she turned to Bertha and demanded, "What did you say to make her cry? Wait until Ty hears about this. He won't be very pleased with you, Bertha."

Irma's certainty that Ty would leap to her defense made the tears well anew in Mary Ellen's eyes.

"See?" Irma faced Bertha accusingly. "You should be ashamed of yourself, Bertha! Ty is going to be furious."

"Mr. Stevenson has left the tour," Bertha retorted.

"Left?" Irma was stunned by the news. "Why?"

Bertha repeated Mary Ellen's words: "Something came up."

"This doesn't make sense," Sheldon said, joining the conversation for the first time. "Why would Ty leave before the tour was over? Was it something to do with his job?"

Mary Ellen latched on to the excuse. "Yes."

"He's all right, though?" Irma asked her.

Mary Ellen nodded.

"Well, it's a real shame he had to leave

early," Irma murmured, "but you'll be seeing him again soon."

No, I won't. It's over, Mary Ellen told herself. *And standing here making a spectacle of yourself isn't going to change that.*

"I'll be fine," Mary Ellen told Irma with uncharacteristic coolness. She was angry at having broken down in front of everyone and acting like an hysterical idiot. "I'd really prefer not to talk about it anymore."

As she boarded the bus she was very much aware of the curious looks being given to Ty's empty seat. No one said anything to her, though. Apparently Irma had spread the word that Ty had left and that Mary Ellen wasn't to be questioned about it. For that Mary Ellen was grateful.

She couldn't stop the memories—memories of last night and the wonder of making love with Ty. But she forced herself to remember the way Ty had left her twice before. And to recall that he hadn't denied it when she'd said the time had come for him to return to Monte Carlo. He'd merely objected to the timing.

Mary Ellen cynically decided that timing is what made or broke relationships. Each time she'd been ready to give herself, Ty hadn't been ready to commit himself. It had been too soon for him, and it was now too late for her. Timing.

The bus stopped for lunch, but Mary Ellen couldn't eat. She didn't know the name of the town they were in, or even the country. Had they left France for Belgium yet? It didn't seem important.

She aimlessly wandered around the narrow streets of wherever-they-were until it was time to board the bus again.

"Brussels is the headquarters of the European Common Market," Mitzi told her in an attempt to cheer her up.

Mary Ellen didn't care.

"How about joining Hank and me for dinner later tonight?" Viola suggested.

Mary Ellen turned her down. She didn't want to tinge Viola's newfound happiness with her own despair.

Archie seemed to be the only one who understood. He silently offered her the use of his Walkman.

Mary Ellen accepted, and used the music to block out her painful thoughts.

Back in Paris Ty had his own painful thoughts to overcome and was finally responding to the handful of messages he'd been given at the desk when he'd left the hotel. The messages were all from Lars.

"Ty! I was getting worried that you hadn't called. Did you get my messages?"

"Yes."

"I've got important news," Lars began.

"You're going to tell me that our cardsharp friend is dead, correct?"

"Correct. How did you hear about it?" Lars asked him.

"I saw it in the papers here in Paris."

"What about Pierre and Josef?"

"We came to an agreement," Ty replied.

"What kind of an agreement?"

Lars was once again flabbergasted by Ty's explanation of events. "That's as wild as the episode in the cuckoo clock factory. You've blackmailed Pierre and Josef into doing charity work? Unbelievable! This woman of yours must really be something to have affected you so much. I can't wait to meet her. How are things going between you two, anyway?"

"They're not going very well at the moment," Ty admitted.

The unusual sound of rough defeat in Ty's voice disturbed Lars. "Don't give up, my friend. From what you've told me of Marielle, she sounds like a woman worth fighting for."

"She is."

"Then fight for her."

Determination replaced defeat as Ty stated, "I intend to."

"That's the spirit. Good luck," Lars offered.

"Thanks. I have a feeling I may need it."

By this time Mary Ellen and the rest of the tour group had arrived in Brussels. Mary Ellen really tried to come out of her depression and take an interest in the sights she was being shown on the city tour. But it was useless.

Here she was, sitting at a table with a cheerful group of people—Irma, Sheldon, Mitzi, Viola, Hank, and Archie—at a cafe in the middle of the city's Grand Place. She should be feeling something.

"My guidebook says that the Grand Place is one of the finest squares in Europe." The comment came from Mitzi.

"That's what your guidebook said about the square in Copenhagen," Archie claimed.

Mary Ellen remembered the square in Copenhagen, the one where Ty had first approached her about joining her tour.

Mitzi checked her guidebook. "No, my guidebook didn't say that about Copenhagen."

"Christian told us that," Hank recalled.

"That's right," Viola agreed. "And it was lovely. You really can't make comparisons. I think everything we've seen on this tour has been beautiful on its own behalf."

"This square sure is something, though," Sheldon said as he took yet another photograph of the surrounding buildings that dated as far back as the fifteenth century. "Hey, is it my imagination or does the left side of the town hall look wider than the right side?"

"It's not your imagination," Mitzi assured Sheldon. "The two sides were built at different times. There's supposed to be an excellent view of the city from the top, but according to my guidebook, you have to climb four hundred and twenty steps to get up there."

"I think I'll pass on that," Sheldon declared. "I'm too comfortable sitting here watching the people go by."

The people didn't interest Mary Ellen, because none of them were Ty. History did not repeat itself; Ty didn't appear out of nowhere and announce his intention of joining her. Ty wasn't going to appear in her life ever again. She had to cut her losses and go on.

But how? she wondered in the loneliness of her hotel room that night. Her sense of loss was enormous as she grieved over the shattered dream of sharing her life with the man who had consumed her heart, her mind, her soul. Because once and for all she'd buried any hopes she'd had of their having a future together. She'd spent more than seven years waiting; that was long enough.

Another gust of pain rocked her, intensifying the headache that plowed through her skull and banged at her temples. Why? Why couldn't it have been different? Why did it have to end this way?

The questions, the doubts, the hurt, seized her and kept her in their grasp throughout that long, sleepless night. In the morning Mary Ellen was so tired that she only wanted the tour to be over. The weather was gray and dismal as the bus took the group to Ostend to catch the ferry boat across the Channel to England.

During the choppy ride across the Channel the group's conversation inevitably turned to thoughts of the future, as the end of their trip drew nearer.

"I'm going to sign up for my next vacation as soon as I get home," Mitzi told them. "That way I won't get depressed because this trip will be over. How does an escorted bus tour of Japan sound?"

"Sheldon and I took one last year," Irma replied. "We enjoyed it. We're thinking of visiting Rio during Carnival season for our next vacation. What about you, Viola?"

Viola turned to Hank, as if seeking his advice.

Hank replied on her behalf. "I've invited Viola to visit Archie and me during her next school break. She's never been to the States."

Irma practically beamed. "How wonderful!" She was so pleased to see Hank and Viola looking so happy. Now if only there were a way to cheer up Mary Ellen. But Irma had a feeling that Ty Stevenson was the only one who'd be able to do that.

When Mary Ellen checked into the hotel in London, she was told that an important message had been left for her. "I was instructed to give this to you as soon as you arrived," the desk clerk said before handing her a folded piece of paper.

For a moment Mary Ellen feared that the message might concern Ty, and she frantically wondered if she'd ever be free. But the message was from Jennifer.

Arrangements have already been made for our tea at the Ritz. See you there today at four.

Mary Ellen had completely forgotten her agreement to have a repeat of their earlier tea engagement. At the time it had seemed like it would be fun, seeing Jennifer one more time before leaving England. But now Mary Ellen didn't consider it to be such a wonderful idea. So she called Jennifer, hoping to catch her friend before she left.

"Jennifer, it's Mary Ellen. Look, I'm sorry, but I don't think I can make our tea date this afternoon."

"Oh, Mary Ellen, don't cancel out on me now! I've been so looking forward to it. After all, this is the last time I'll be seeing you for a while. You fly back to the States tomorrow, don't you?"

"Yes."

"Then this is the last time we'll be able to get together."

"Jennifer, I just don't think it's a good idea."

"Why not?"

Mary Ellen got right to the point, although she was so upset that she had some difficulty framing the words. "I've broken things off with Ty. I don't want to talk about him."

"If that's the way you feel, then we won't talk about him."

"Jennifer, he's your brother."

"So?"

"So . . ."

Jennifer interrupted Mary Ellen's floundering explanation. "Look, would it help if I promised not to discuss Ty at all, not to even mention his name? I wasn't the one who brought him up today, you know. You were."

"All right, under that condition I'll meet you.

I'm sorry for being—" Once again Mary Ellen was broken off by Jennifer.

"Never mind," Jennifer cheerfully retorted. "What are good friends for if you can't abuse them? Just be at the Ritz at four."

"I will."

It felt strange walking back into the formidable lobby that had so intimidated her when Mary Ellen had first arrived in London. That had only been two weeks ago, yet it felt like two years. She'd changed. And so had the snooty maître d'.

Oh, the man was the same one who'd looked down his nose at her before. But his attitude was completely different.

"May I help you?" he inquired with polite deference.

"I'm here to meet someone for tea. Jennifer Ashford."

"Of course, madam. Right this way."

She was immediately shown to a table and treated with lavish attention. The maître d' held out her chair for her and unfolded her napkin with a flourish. A waiter handed her a tea menu while another waiter poured a glass of ice water for her. Surrounded as she was by such attentive minions, it took Mary Ellen a moment or two to realize that she was the only patron present.

The area reserved for the serving of tea would normally seat at least fifty people. But the other tables were all covered with carnations, red carnations. Hundreds of them! Obviously someone was planning a private celebration here and had reserved the area exclusively.

"There must be some mistake," Mary Ellen told the maître d'.

He shook his head, but his reply was drowned out by the sound of violins. Mary Ellen peered around the waiter, who was still fussing with her water glass, and saw a string of violinists playing their hearts out. The music was vaguely familiar, but she couldn't place it.

"We danced to this while cruising down the River Seine in Paris. Remember, Marielle?"

It couldn't be. It was. Ty.

Although it had only been two days since she'd last seen him, Ty had changed. It wasn't merely that he'd forsaken his battered leather jacket for a more traditional Harris Tweed. There was something different about his attitude. The reckless gleam normally lighting his brown eyes was absent, and instead she viewed what almost appeared to be a shadow of uncertainty. Surely that must be a trick of the lighting, for Ty was never uncertain.

Hard though it was, Mary Ellen tore her gaze away from Ty and focused instead on her surroundings. The red carnations, the romantic music, Jennifer's insistence that she wouldn't discuss Ty—it all fell into place. She'd been set up. "You and Jennifer planned this, didn't you? She never intended on showing up for tea this afternoon, did she?" Mary Ellen couldn't help but feel betrayed.

"Now, Marielle, don't blame Jen. She was only showing some pity for her heartbroken older brother," Ty murmured with a half-hearted grin as he joined Mary Ellen at the table, sitting across from her.

"And blood is thicker than water, right?"

The bitterness in her voice chased any sign of humor from his face. "Jennifer would never have agreed to become involved in this scheme if she didn't believe it was in your best interest as well as my own. She's still your loyal friend."

"You talked her into helping you," Mary Ellen accused him. "She knew I didn't want to see you."

"She knows I love you," Ty quietly replied.

His words made Mary Ellen falter. For one brief moment her heart leapt with hope, only to fall like a stone. He'd told her before that he loved her. He'd left anyway. She knew to her own regret that love and commitment did not go hand in hand with Ty.

She shook her head with defeated resignation. "It's not enough, Ty."

He stiffened, anger compressing his lips into a grim line. "What's that supposed to mean?"

"It means that we have different ideas of love. For me it means commitment and fidelity, for you it means—"

"That I want to marry you," he inserted in an authoritative voice.

Now Mary Ellen's heartbeat did go crazy.

She could hardly breathe. "What did . . . you say?"

"That I want to marry you," he repeated, more softly this time.

She looked stunned, disbelieving. "Why?"

Ty looked relieved that she hadn't given him an immediate refusal. "There are a lot of reasons. But before I go on, I need to know something. Why did you send me away in Paris?"

"I couldn't take having you leave me a third time," she admitted in a husky voice. "You never gave me a sign that what we shared was anything more than a good time while I was here in Europe. You never hinted that once the vacation was over, our affair wouldn't be over too."

"It will never be over between us, Marielle. You may have known it before I did, but I've learned the lesson well. Believe me." He leaned forward to thread his fingers through hers. "I want us to be together." He lifted her hand to his lips. "Always. That's one of the reasons I want to marry you. But it's not the only reason. You already know I want you, I've told you that I love you and need you." Ty was getting desperate. "What do I have to say to convince you?"

"Tell me about the Grand Prix racing circuit."

Her non sequitur threw him. "What?"

"A wife should know what her husband does for a living, don't you agree?"

The gleam returned to his dark eyes. "You're saying yes? You will marry me?"

"Yes. I will marry you."

Ty gave a triumphant shout, leapt from his seat, and whisked Mary Ellen up into his arms.

"Ty! What are you doing?"

"Celebrating."

"Here?"

"Upstairs."

"Ty, put me down," she frantically requested. "I'm sure the Ritz frowns on this sort of display."

"I'm sure they do. And, frankly, my dear, I don't give a damn," he quoted. "I finally got up enough nerve to ask the woman I love to marry me, and she's accepted! I intend to enjoy every moment of it."

"Ty . . ." Her voice grew less disapproving as the joy of being in his arms again overrode all else. "They're going to kick us out of here for causing a scene."

"No, they're not," he assured her as he carried her past the disbelieving maître d' to the elevators in the hotel lobby. "It helps when your brother-in-law is the new manager of the place."

"Jennifer's husband?"

"He's the only brother-in-law I have," Ty replied while giving a polite nod to the wide-eyed matron who had just gotten off the elevator.

"That's how you arranged to have the entire

section reserved with the flowers and the musicians?"

"That's right." Ty finally set Mary Ellen back on her feet when they entered the elevator. "Jennifer made me promise to call her later. She was afraid you might never speak to her again," he said as the elevator whisked them up to the top floor. Taking Mary Ellen by the hand he led her to the door of what turned out to be a luxurious suite. "She told me you sounded miserable when she spoke to you earlier."

"I was miserable without you," she murmured as Ty closed the door behind them, shutting out the rest of the world.

"Then you'll never be miserable again," he promised her, "because you won't be without me again." He held her to him, gathering her closer as if she might break. Ty had always been a very physical man, his body language telling her more than his words often did. The tenderness of his embrace was intense.

She tightened her arms around him. Still in awe of this newfound happiness, she tried to address the last remnants of her uncertainty. "Ty, did you really mean it, what you said about marrying me?"

"I was never more serious in my life. I know you don't think I'm the marrying kind, but haven't you heard that reformed rakes make the best husbands?" He drew her face away from his shoulder and cupped it with gentle hands. "I want to make you happy, I want to be the best husband in the world for you."

She brought his hands to her lips so that she could kiss the hands that had given her so much pleasure. "You asked me a question after we made love in Frankfurt. I didn't answer it then, but I want to now." She raised her eyes, those expressive eyes that had always told him what she really felt. She looked directly at him as she spoke. "You were my first lover, and you've been my only lover." She could see the impact her words had on him. His appreciation and satisfaction were evident.

He spoke her name with the rough gentleness she knew and loved so well. "Marielle . . ."

But she wasn't done yet, not by a long shot. "You don't have to worry about being the best husband in the world for me," she told him as she slid her hands beneath his Harris Tweed jacket. "Because you're the *only* man in the world for me."

"I don't deserve you," he muttered. "But I don't plan on questioning my luck. I've thought it all out. There's a Hunger Prevention office in Monaco, within driving distance of where I live. You won't have to give up your work if you don't want to."

Mary Ellen was deeply touched by his forethought, and it cemented her conviction that Ty had indeed given their future together a great deal of consideration. This was no spur-of-the-moment, flash-in-the-pan idea. As he'd said, it may have taken him longer to get to the point of commitment, but now that he was there he had no doubts about it. And neither did she. Not anymore.

"Did you bring me up here to discuss my work?" she asked him with a saucy grin.

"Ac-tu-al-ly . . ." He drew the word out, emphasizing each syllable as he carefully untied the silk scarf from its neat bow beneath her blouse's collar. The swishing sound of silk sliding over silk was a provocative preview of things to come. "Now that you mention it . . ." Again he paused, this time to unbutton her blouse with careful deliberation. "I did have another activity in mind."

"Activity, huh?"

"Mmmm." He kissed the base of her throat and the pulse beating there. "It's a rather popular indoor sport." His kisses slid over her bared shoulders as he slipped the blouse down her arms and tossed it onto a chair.

"No special equipment needed?" Her sexy inquiry was both breathless and sultry.

"No." Ty removed her bra and gazed at her for a moment of mute appreciation. "You've got all the equipment anyone could need or want," he told her in a husky undertone.

"There's just one problem."

"I know." He smoothed her hair away from her bare shoulders and kissed the tip of her ear. "You're scheduled to fly home tomorrow morning." He drew away to give her a reassuring grin. "Don't worry, I plan on rejoining your tour group in time to fly back with you. Can you imagine the look on *my mother*'s face when I tell her I'm getting married?"

"She'll be astonished, I'm sure." She arched her neck to allow him better access to the hollows of her throat. "But that wasn't the problem I was referring to."

Her words halted his nuzzling progress. "There's another problem?"

She nodded.

"What is it?" He looked concerned—distracted, but concerned.

Mary Ellen's grin could have matched one of his for devilishness as she reached for him. "Your equipment is still covered up."

He groaned as her playfulness became more intimate. "You ain't seen nothin' yet!"

"I know." Her laugh was husky and soft. "That's what I'm complaining about."

He moved away from her bewitching fingers and hastily stripped. "Then I'll just have to make sure that you don't have anything to complain about." He tugged her back into his arms and removed the remainder of her clothing with equal rapidity. "In fact"—he cupped her breasts in the palms of his hands—"I intend to make that my lifetime occupation."

"Lifetime?" The glow in her eyes was radiant. "I like the sound of that."

"How about the feel of this?" He moved against her.

"Mmmmmm, show me more."

"It'll be my pleasure."

"It'll be *our* pleasure," she corrected him. It was.

Catch up with any

Candlelights

you're missing.

Here are the Ecstasies published this past May

ECSTASY SUPREMES $2.75 each

☐ 121 **BEYOND A DOUBT**, Eleanor Woods 10655-9-24
☐ 122 **TORCH SONG**, Lee Magner 18718-4-22
☐ 123 **CUPID'S DILEMMA**, Ginger Chambers . . 11632-5-46
☐ 124 **A FRAGILE DECEPTION**, Jane Atkin 12695-9-30

ECSTASY ROMANCES $2.25 each

☐ 426 **FANTASY LOVER**, Anne Silverlock 12438-7-73
☐ 427 **PLAYING WITH FIRE**, Donna Kimel Vitek . 16983-6-81
☐ 428 **JUST A LOT MORE TO LOVE**, Lynn Patrick 14409-4-25
☐ 429 **HOT ON HIS TRAIL**, Lori Copeland 13777-2-13
☐ 430 **PRISONER OF PASSION**, Suzannah Davis 17110-5-28
☐ 431 **LOVE MAKES THE DIFFERENCE**,
           Emily Elliott 13774-8-32
☐ 432 **ROOM FOR TWO**, Joan Grove 17476-7-34
☐ 433 **THE BITTER WITH THE SWEET**,
           Alison Tyler 10583-8-21

At your local bookstore or use this handy coupon for ordering:

Dell **DELL READERS SERVICE—DEPT. B1150A**
          P.O. BOX 1000, PINE BROOK, N.J. 07058

Please send me the above title(s). I am enclosing $_____$ (please add 75¢ per copy to cover postage and handling). Send check or money order - no cash or CODs. Please allow 3-4 weeks for shipment.
CANADIAN ORDERS: please submit in U.S. dollars.

Ms Mrs Mr_____

Address_____

City State_____ Zip _____

VV5
+1
+8